They More than Burned

by

Tara Stillions Whitehead

ELJ Editions, Ltd. is committed to publishing works of quality and integrity. In that spirit, we are proud to offer this story collection to our readers. This is a work of fiction. Names, characters, places, and incidents either are the product of the author's imagination or are used fictitiously, and any resemblance to actual persons, living or dead, business establishments, events, or locales is entirely coincidental.

ISBN: 978-1-942004-53-0

Library of Congress Control Number: 2022951827

Cover Design by Justin Stillions
Cover Art "San Diego Beach"
(https://pixabay.com/photos/san-diego-beach-ocean-5188311/)

ELJ Editions, Ltd.
P.O. Box 815
Washingtonville, NY 10992

www.elj-editions.com

Praise for *They More Than Burned*

"Whitehead spins epic stories of addiction and recovery in tiny spaces, recovered memories and lives over 20 years and 2,900 miles. The book's closing lines define its resonance: 'You will pick it up and hold it to your chest. You will scream my name.' Readers of this collection will do the same—hold the words close and remember her name." – Amy Barnes, author of *Child Craft*

"*They More Than Burned* is an incendiary archive: a collection of jagged memories that tumble and catch one another in the light, an unwinding a spool of film on fire. Whitehead narrates the fire of a burning world—Southern California wildfires, the burning of the Twin Towers, a house set ablaze and filmed—but the real fire in question throughout this book is the passion of this woman who, at sixteen, began to film a generation as it emerged in the shadow of these fires, a product of the gritty Southern California reality where parents are in prison, boys go from being anarchists to soldiers overnight, and going back to the beginning is painful because that's when everyone was still alive. To bring their lost faces to light, she persists refusing to be dimmed by exploitative Hollywood bosses, sleazy post-me-too producers, and addiction and its terrible consequences.

Southern California's Gogol, Whitehead records the diary of not a madwoman, but a woman made mad. Watch as Whitehead burns it down, and rejoice at the power of her will and the power of her words." – Katie Farris, author of *Standing in the Forest of Being Alive*

for Jenn

Drive

The last day I see you alive, you eat dim sum for breakfast and show me your Galaxie—press my pale thighs against its Phoenician yellow and Navajo white. You kiss me like you used to kiss your wife before she was your wife and leave me wondering if you taste like Djarum Blacks when you apologize to her on Mondays.

The last day I see you alive, you smell like morning surf and patchouli, an entire summer of want. We split a piece of Big Red and drive to Tanglehood where you fix the pickup on Bill's guitar, break his E string while playing "Rivers of Babylon," apologize to the cat, clear the bong chamber, draw tiny infinities on my ankle with a Sharpie, and cry about the letter you got from Joe.

You're done chasing prostitutes in GTA by noon and need to go Downtown, so you invite Bill, let him ride shotgun because he doesn't talk much and has a pompadour. You pick up AJ, pick up Danny, pick up Shawntá. You cruise Tamarack while we finger the chrome ashtrays and lie cool against the polished leather doors. You pop a CD adapter into the cassette deck and play the mix Kim made for you, skip "40 oz. to Freedom" to "Disarm," park across from Spin Records, next the white gazebo—a premiere parking space in Downtown. You shepherd us through the parking lot, sing about how we can't all stay here forever in that Shannon Hoon register I've never heard before.

Everyone goes to the bar while we get stoned with Josh in the Village bathroom. You whisper about Joe and the war. The desert is in your voice. You spin me out of the stall, across the walkway to Vinaka, claim the last iron patio chair on the over-deck. You light a clove, send moon-shaped smoke signals into the cafe umbrella. You eat biscotti, laugh at the tourists, visit the payphone by the souvenir shop downstairs, and come back a little taller, brighter, a little less saturnine.

The last day I see you alive, you ask me about film school. Have I met George Lucas yet? You tell me you've been putting your portfolio together. You ask what it's like to challenge the legacy of old white men whose names gold-plate the university sound stages I've been losing myself in.

You tell me I need to put the Galaxie in a movie.

"Producers drop hella cash for picture cars," I say. "It's easy. All you do is drive."

I'm smart, not beautiful, and I've never had a man tell me he wants to run away with me without telling me he wants to run away with me before.

I'm still so young.

You stop asking questions about film school. You get up, go down to the payphone, come back with two cups of black coffee. I want to take a picture of the steam rising to meet your freckled lips, the way your entire body curses the sun. But I've left my camera on a closet shelf in my LA bedroom, convinced this place from my past is a secret I can visit and escape as I please.

Before you go to work, you swap your clove for charcoal, draw Rob's portrait on a napkin, tell Emily about the letter her brother sent, pull your accoutrements—pristine, white, creaseless—out of your Jansport backpack. You walk around the corner singing "Hunger Strike," spend four hours slinging halibut, veal, endless bowls of calamari. You bless everything with your special sauce, drink the scotch women your mother's age buy you, and slip their numbers in the trash.

At four o'clock, you pack your apron away, change back into Catholic black, return to find me and Jake rolling cigarettes. You take us to Peabody's, buy the bar a round of your Irish beer, play Eightball, stack coasters, do a speed bump with some Pendleton jarheads, leave, use the payphone, come back, shove bills into the jukebox, play Jenn's favorite songs, lick Anita's tits behind the air hockey table, pose for Kim's Nikon, sweep your curls and flex your dragon. You find the shadows, watch me watching you watch Bob watching me, orbiting like a moon, feeding me two shots of Goldschläger, grabbing my arm. You know what Bob did to Janae—we all know—so you breeze over, put your inked-up fingers in the back pocket of my cutoffs, give me the keys to the Galaxie.

We float down serpentine streets to the lagoon, to a man-sized hole in the chain link. You make yourself weightless above my body, the spectral chamise, say you're running away with me in the morning, say you don't want to be twenty-two forever.

In a few weeks, during peak fire season, I'll regret the ecstasy of coming while thinking about going, slipping away from you, the chaparral, the summer, into the last-week memory of sleeping with my Film Studies TA in the reference stacks of Doheny Library.

"They shot *Ghostbusters* here," he'd whispered into the damp shell of my ear. Then, "Don't tell anyone, but I never finished Kurosawa's *Dreams*."

I'm passing Dana Point on the 5 North by seven, half drunk, half shaking, one hundred percent alive and moving away, into the brightening every next second of my life, the holy ghost of you singing inside of me.

The last time I see you and your Galaxie, it's on a

screen that's not showing one of my movies.

You've stopped leaving Monty Python recordings on my voicemail, stopped texting about Joe's letters, about the babies and the divorce, the sun's unbearable ennui, and whether I could put in a good word about your Roski Art School application.

I'm about to leave my bungalow a mile north of the university on 27th and Hoover, am bracing myself for the 5's gridlock and thinking about white leather and chrome, anticipating the sound of rain on the hard top, the eventual relief in your face. I'm walking through the garden gate towards the alley when Shawntá calls me and says, "Go back inside," says, "turn on the TV," says, "you see that fire?" says, "that's all that's left of JP and the Galaxie."

That was how I loved you in the end.   With my body cold and shuddering. With empty hands over smoldering ash, counting out the minutes.

- from "In the End" by Lang Leav

How to Begin the Unfinished Documentary About Your Life

(Feature Film Treatment, rev. 9/25/21)

LOGLINE: A promising young filmmaker facing addiction and the early end to her Hollywood career discovers a box of lost interviews and embarks on the project of a lifetime.

ACT I

Sc. 0 - 1
ENTER THE WORLD like a monsoon in April. Refuse to blink. Reject sleep. Screech like a stone kettle when you are placed on your back and left alone in the dark. You don't understand it yet, but you were born afraid you will miss something.

Sc. 2 - 3
Walk before you crawl. In fact, never crawl at all. Speak in tongues before you receive the sacrament. Invent names for the voices of ghosts you HEAR but cannot see. Construct a cinematic universe of play where the ghosts are your biological family. SING to them at five octaves higher than your speaking voice. Claim it is the register of the Lord. Believe that the world is inherently good. Believe that your survival is in its best interest.

Believe that your survival is a kind of performance you will spend your whole life trying to master.

Sc. 4 - 6
Cope with adolescence by constantly auditioning for a better life. Discover early on that a body needs protection. Fast legs. Complicated fasteners. Powerful lungs. Pretend a stomach full of sick feelings is a form of currency. Abandonment. Addiction. Betrayal.

[redacted]

"Trauma is an investment," they will tell you in auditions. "It's what gives you range."

Sc. 7
Because you were born afraid you will miss something, document everything. Keep inventory using NOTEBOOKS and HARD DRIVES and TAPES. Continue doing this upon reaching adulthood. Continue doing this when you move to LA to attend THE MOST FAMOUS FILM SCHOOL IN THE WORLD.

Sc. 8
Drink a lot of cheap wine while studying at THE MOST FAMOUS FILM SCHOOL IN THE WORLD. Sleep with various members of the Thornton School of Music. Tuba Dan. The

Prince fanatic with two drum sets and an iso booth in his campus apartment. The whispery Texan you ask to score your junior thesis. Feel simultaneously exhilarated and panicked about attending THE MOST FAMOUS FILM SCHOOL IN THE WORLD. Make out with famous people's kids. Try cocaine and German expressionism. The latter isn't for you. Make a lot of dark and alienated -- borderline pornographic -- films and screen them without closing your eyes. See how much you can get away with. Worry that, no matter how good you are, your body will be used as a bartering tool for someone else's success.

Sc. 9 - 13
Graduate from THE MOST FAMOUS FILM SCHOOL IN THE WORLD with a fatty liver and malnourished ego. Take the first production job you can get. Find it on Craigslist. Realize that THE MOST FAMOUS FILM SCHOOL IN THE WORLD did not prepare you for twenty-hour days and low-budget conditions. But stick with it. You can't quit now. Not when your student loans are about to go into repayment. Not when classmates from high school are ODing and hanging themselves in their parents' garages. Work really hard to get into the DIRECTORS GUILD OF AMERICA and, once you are finally in the DIRECTORS GUILD OF AMERICA, leave the DIRECTORS GUILD OF

AMERICA for a job that can give you that better life you've been waiting for: a job in sitcoms.

Sc. 14
Discover that the most tormented people in the entertainment industry work in sitcoms.

Sc. 15
Quit Hollywood before the cops find your dismembered body parts wrapped in CINEFOIL and scattered like EASTER EGGS around the GRIFFITH PARK CAROUSEL. Be sure to save the emails and text messages and detailed accounts of your abuse —— the VP of HR's impenetrable silence —— before you turn in your badge and leave the studio lot for the last time. You won't know it's the last time, and it's better that way.

Sc. 16 - 17
Lose all words for what happened behind the cameras, inside producers' Priuses, beneath the flesh you want peel yourself out of so that you could find a new, better self. Spend three months and a twenty-third birthday collecting unemployment, pendulating between pathological alcoholism and obsessively researching botched lethal injections for a feature script you are writing.

Sc. 18
During one of the pathological alcoholism phases, meet the HANDSOME PENNSYLVANIA HIGH SCHOOL TEACHER at a dive bar in a Los Feliz strip mall. Compliment him on his Pennsylvania Big Foot Society T-shirt. Describe his eyes as sacred blue. Interpret this to mean he will save you when the time comes to be saved. Listen to him with an attentiveness you didn't know you had, but only remember big-picture details, like that he's trying to move to California and has an interview in Hemet, that his cousin lives a mile from the second-floor apartment you share with an anorexic stand-up comedian behind the Church of Scientology building on Hollywood Boulevard. Tell him that Hemet is a shit hole. Promptly apologize for dashing his dreams. Kiss him in the McDonald's drive thru on Sunset and then let him feel you up on the deck of his cousin's yurt in Silverlake. Do not panic until he calls the next day, asking to kiss you again.

Sc. 19 - 23
When the HANDSOME PENNSYLVANIA HIGH SCHOOL TEACHER doesn't get the job in Hemet, fly to Pittsburgh to attend his friend's wedding. Give him a blow job on the turnpike and return to LA in existential crisis. Spend hours leaning your head

against the cold plaster of each wall in your apartment behind the Church of Scientology building. Realize that the only joy you feel is when the HANDSOME PENNSYLVANIA HIGH SCHOOL TEACHER sends cryptic love notes like "without wax." Play PJ Harvey's "White Chalk" on repeat while earthquakes try to level your apartment behind the Church of Scientology building. Call the HANDSOME PENNSYLVANIA HIGH SCHOOL TEACHER after he has taken Benadryl to fall asleep. Ask if his beagle misses you. Ask if he's ever hiked the Appalachian Trail. Ask if he really believes in Bigfoot. Find yourself constantly thinking about the swamp cooler in his bedroom window, how the damp smell it left on everything reminded you of your grandmother's lake house, the one that disappeared in a wildfire, the last place you were child.

Sc. 24
Plan to drink yourself to death.

Sc. 25 - 28
Avoid drinking yourself to death by spending a month on set with a UPM who wants you to rejoin the DIRECTOR'S GUILD OF AMERICA. Find relief in being too busy to look at yourself in a mirror. Work eighteen-hour days on the Paramount lot off of Santa Monica Boulevard and fall

asleep during phone sex with the HANDSOME PENNSYLVANIA HIGH SCHOOL TEACHER. Try to avoid a long-distance relationship with him at all costs by explaining that your neglected dreams need you. Tell him you are still in mourning. Tell him you require a lot of alone time. Tell him you can't live without him. Tell him your deepest fear: that you will never finish this screenplay or have the better life you've been looking for. Tell him that sitcom writers are monstrous people who will steal everything from you. And then tell him exactly how they did it.

Sc. 29
After three months of phone sex and mailing each other emotionally esoteric CD mixes, accept -- much to your disappointment -- that you have fallen in love with the HANDSOME PENNSYLVANIA HIGH SCHOOL TEACHER. Enter another existential crisis. Tell your UPM friend at Paramount that you woke up with mono and can't work. Call your HANDSOME PENNSYLVANIA HIGH SCHOOL TEACHER when he gets off of bus duty. Suggest leaving LA immediately and moving in with him. Feel terror creep into your body when he says yes and that he wanted it to be your idea.

Sc. 30 - 33
Sell or give away everything that doesn't

fit into your 1997 4-Runner, and journey America's 2,900-mile waistline alone. It takes four days. Because it is October, everything north and east of the Mississippi is exploding with colors you've only seen on TV. Realize how much of the world you missed while creating a world you can only see on TV.

Sc. 34 - 37
Live quietly for a year in a town that drops a wrench from the sky every New Year's Eve. Sit on porches. Eat perogies with butter. Make love during thunderstorms and discover that fireflies are real. Collect your California unemployment until someone hires you for temp work. Drive into the city twice a week to sell plasma. Get engaged to the HANDSOME PENNSYLVANIA HIGH SCHOOL TEACHER. Apply for graduate school in California. Get accepted into graduate school in California. Move into a granny flat on top of a DESERT MOUNTAIN and make daily 6am hikes to the top to marvel at the ocean you missed while you were in the town that drops a wrench every New Year's Eve. Try to drink a little less. Try to forget Hollywood and sitcoms and the hours of tape you've shot but never cut. Convince yourself you're a writer now, not a filmmaker. No one uses tape anymore anyway.

ACT II

Sc. 38
Go HOME. Even if it doesn't feel like
HOME. Even if you've spent the last ten
years recovering from the idea of HOME.
Pretend it's just another film set. A tiny
sound stage built to house your infinite
shame. Imagine the people inside are
ACTORS waiting for your direction. Try not
to think too much about the GRIEF your
LOVE for them has become.

Sc. 39
Exit 5 North at Tamarack instead of Elm.
Drive Highland along the lagoon, past the
house Tony Hawk lived in when he could
still land tricks, past the hole in the
fence you and the boys from YELLOW HOUSE
used to drag wood pallets through for
nighttime bonfires. The estuary's stench
of sulphur and rotting kelp will remind
you of getting lit, getting laid, getting
overcome by your own ridiculous heat. Let
it.

Sc. 40
Once you get to Park Drive, turn left.
Swing around the south side of the high
school, which is still a long, gray wall
with purple and gold painted gates at each
end. Pass over El Camino Real, and just
like every other time you did when you

lived here, remember how the King's Highway runs 500 miles north, ending not too far past Patty's Inn, the bar your grandmother tended until it burned to the ground. You cannot count how many places you've been that have burned to the ground.

Sc. 41
Park one driveway down from the house you grew up in. You won't be here long, but you don't want to get a ticket for parking in front of the fire hydrant that has existed specifically to perplex your father on days when he brought home cars from the shop.

Sc. 41 (CONT'D)
Take long, sure-footed steps towards ███, the house number still listed on your student loan statements and Director's Guild of America pension. Hesitate at the driveway's threshold long enough to notice what is missing. The dwarf palm trees and Bird of Paradise. The wicker rocker and the ashtrays and the crack in the cement porch you once filled with hot glue and Kool Aid. Don't make yourself sick over the fresh landscape of pepper gravel and solar lights. The house is better maintained now that you and your siblings have been scattered by the winds of adulthood. It might not feel like it, but

this is a good thing.

Sc. 42
Walk the short driveway where you once
kissed a homecoming date who, months
later, botched an elaborate plot to kill
you and place you in cement behind the
carport at his mom's modular home.

Sc. 42 (CONT'D)
Reach the porch where you spent countless
San Diego afternoons smoking Marlboro
Ultra Lights with your stepmother and
waiting for the phone to ring, for Nikki
or Janae or Joe or one of the Yellow House
boys to invite you Downtown. Notice the
absence of ash and long white filters.
Recognize the guilt you harbor for missing
those two years she slept through
interferon treatments -- for being drunk
the last day you saw her mother alive. You
didn't know you were arguing with the
brain tumor that turned her tongue into
acid. The Tito's in your gut had
transformed you into a black hole.

Set all of this aside for now.

Write it down when you get back to the
granny flat you share with your fiancé on
the DESERT MOUNTAIN near the university.
You will need it in five years when you
get sober for the second time and your

sponsor tells you to stop dragging your feet on the ninth step.

Sc. 42 (CONT'D) /43
Knock and enter. Don't wait for someone to open the door. You may have spent a decade running away from this place, but you can't pretend that you don't know the door is always unlocked for you. Let this small truth neutralize the emotional maelstrom that has been forming in your gut during the 40-minute drive from the desert to the coast.

Sc. 43 (CONT'D)
Find your father shirtless and asleep on his recliner. Notice how years of oil and grease from other people's cars have transformed the recliner into the hard-worked palm of God. Notice how the hard-worked palm of God cradles your father's aching body, soothes it small and weightless. Feel momentary relief. Then, dread. How close in age you have become.

Sc. 44
Search the garage for the pile your father made. Dig through the YEARBOOKS and BAR COASTERS and FOLDED NOTES from long gone friends -- Nikki, Anita, Kelsey, and Shoshona -- let their song lyrics and existential quotations singe your fingertips -- Ilene's Social D, Janae's

Jim Morrison, Jared's Smashing Pumpkins and Goethe. Remember that paper fires are the briefest form of flame but make good kindling for a long, slow burn. Find the MINI DV and HI-8 TAPES at the bottom of the one cardboard box that wasn't destroyed when your stepsister overfilled the washing machine with JNCOs and vomit-caked blankets she brought back from Electric Daisy Carnival. Count TWENTY-FIVE TAPES. Release your held breath. Fire needs air.

Sc. 45
Listen to your father explain the 2008 recession and his fast road to bankruptcy -- a whirlwind two years you've spent leaving Hollywood for Pennsylvania for San Diego for graduate school. Recognize the adult tone he uses to talk about banks and repo and moving to the park where your stepmother owns a double-wide coach. Realize that he has asked you to gather these boxes filled with your life's miscellany not because he doesn't want it anymore, but because IT SHOULD BE SAVED AT ALL COSTS. Who you were, even the person he wasn't always around to see, matters to him.

Sc. 46
Blast Rage Against the Machine for the three miles it takes to travel Elm, past

the cross-streets named after Republican presidents of the 20th Century. When you reach the PCH, where the tourists cross all four corners at once and the light takes forever to change, set your iPod to random. There are so many songs not about summer that remind you of summer and what it was like to not know yourself the way adults are constantly trying to know themselves.

Sc. 46 (CONT'D)
Stop on Incubus even though you've never liked Incubus. You haven't listened to "Drive" since JP crashed his Galaxie, and whenever you're in town, you're thinking of JP. Sitting at the intersection you crossed thousands of times for cigarettes, 40s, carnitas, and the beach, realize that you never stop thinking about JP. You never stop feeling his geography. The entire town is a GHOST MAP you feel in your chest. It keeps the smallest heartaches in motion.

Sc. 47 - 49
Turn left when the protected green tells you to. Pass Cessy's taco shop, Fidel's cantina, the Carlsbad Inn. Think about JP's freckled lips, not the silhouettes of men you followed into ocean-view suites after the bars closed. Hang a left on Walnut. Pull into Dini's. Some of your

high school friends are bartenders here
now, and on a clear evening, you're
guaranteed to see the GREEN FLASH. The
parking lot under the bar is pocket-sized
but do your best to pull into the last
open spot without scraping your 4-Runner
against the yellow pylon.

Sc. 50
Climb the cement stairwell into the SALTY
AIR. Pause next to the scarlet begonias on
the terracotta deck and allow the ocean
breeze to convince you there is a better
life out there.

Sc. 51
Earl is behind the bar. He's just as
pretty as he was in high school when he
went down on you one morning in the
sunroom at Johnboy's parents' house. Sit
at the CORNER STOOL and let a man with
salt-cracked skin and a faded O'Neill
shirt buy you a shot. It's not Tito's, but
it burns in all the right places. Watch
Earl watch the man watch you step out onto
the bustling deck where golden hour
obliterates distinctions between locals
and tourists. Think about the TAPES in the
TRUNK OF YOUR CAR. The gone places. The
interviews. How close you were to your
Hollywood dream once and how you've
learned to live with the hashtag nightmare
now. Try not to think about how many of

the people on those tapes are dead.
Remember instead that you have twenty
minutes of Earl outside Yellow House,
playing hacky sack with JP and Bill.
Remember how, when you asked him what he
thought of the planes crashing into the
World Trade Center, he sang INTO THE LENS,
too close for your Sony's autofocus to
handle: "It's the end of the world as we
know it, and we're all fucked."

Sc. 52
Allow a man who spends more time watching
the surf than riding it to buy you a shot.
Ignore the good-natured texts your fiancé
sends. Ask yourself if the world did end.
Ponder the past twenty years of endings
that have fallen since that day. Calculate
the number of years left until the world
shrinks to absolute nothingness. Do all of
this while accepting drinks from strangers
and bumming half of Earl's pack of Camel
Wides. Do all of this while thinking about
Joe and the war, while old touch and
desire spawn endless B-roll footage,
repopulating your deepest memory. Do all
of this while thinking about Earl and the
sundogs above your open thighs. Do it
while deciding you'll digitize the TAPES
in the TRUNK OF YOUR CAR.

Sc. 53
Whatever you do, don't stop thinking about

those TAPES in the TRUNK OF YOUR CAR. You can't censor the SOUNDS and IMAGES of who you've loved and feared and fucked and forgot. You can try to grieve your loss of longing by sipping reposado under a lilac sky, but an ARCHIVE has already montaged its way into your head, and it's just ENDLESS FOOTAGE of coming and unbecoming, of never quite being, not at ease, not with self, not without sabotage or seaweed or sun sickness. The past will not go away this time.

Sc. 54
Use your filmmaker's eye to frame up THE CROWDED PATIO, Earl at the bar, the faint gold line where the sun entered the sea. This place, these people, full of fire and GREEN FLASH are cinematic in their burning. Even though it could take longer than you think, years beyond the long life you will one day pray for in the middle of the night, you need to do something before they disappear. You need to save the ARCHIVE, the dreams. You need to MAKE THE MOVIE, the book, the whatever it is before you disappear, too.

ACT III

Sc. 55 - 59
Bleed years and money. Have kids who never
sleep, who scream like stone kettles if
you leave them alone in the dark. Stay
sick on the drink. Lose the TAPES and your
Martin guitar somewhere between two cross-
country moves. Argue with ghosts you hear
but cannot see. Spend most of your energy
trying to control people and situations.
Exhaust yourself trying to play God. Write
your will and try not to kill yourself
while searching for the gift of
desperation.

Sc. 60 - 61
One week after crashing your car in a
middle-of-the-night blackout, get sober.
It is harder than you've heard but easier
than you imagined. Give up more than you
want. People, places, anger. Quit writing
and reading and listening to music. Grieve
booze like a lost lover. Recognize that
getting sober is like pulling the plug in
an overfilled bathtub. Emptying is a slow
relief, and the bottom is a hard,
unavoidable truth. Go back to therapy.
Tell the truth. Lose weight. Gain weight.
Struggle with sex and thinking and desire.
Wrestle with boredom. Conclude that
creating anything but empty space has now
become impossible.

Sc. 62 - ?

Relieve boredom. Empty your closets. Empty your drawers. Spend years emptying, finding, discarding the old. Tell yourself you will find yourself once you've erased every trace of the person who built this abandoned empire of shame in your chest. Practice hitting your knees with the intensity you used to reserve for morning screwdrivers. When your husband finds vodka bottles hidden in the ceiling, blame the previous tenant whose bottles you both found when you moved in eight years ago. Go looking for more bottles...but find the TAPES instead. Hesitate long enough for the ADRENALINE to TENDERIZE YOUR BODY. Open the faded rayon camera case and plug the Hi-8 into the VCR your kids use to watch your husband's collection of Disney on VHS. Load the tape marked Tape #1. Slowly lower yourself onto the ottoman your cats use as a scratching post. Let your heart hang in your throat. You're about to FEEL THINGS. You're not sure you can handle feeling things. Feeling things usually makes you want to drink, and you don't know if you're prepared to defend yourself against feeling things. You know that the first tape is going to be the hardest to watch. In the first tape, everyone is still alive.

One More Inch of Shadow

Joe's uncle bought rain barrels and fertilizer. A.J.'s dad emptied the family checking account, $300 at a time, from the Circle K where he bought cartons of cigarettes, where my brother was robbed at gunpoint on Christmas Eve. My stepmom bought a safe and stocked it with Symphony bars, Energizer batteries, and two-way radios.

Before the New Year's Eve party in Crystal's dad's backyard, Anita helped blow up a kiddie pool and fill it with Epsom salt in case the hospitals got too full and her sister, three days past her due date, would have to give birth at home.

Crystal's dad's beach house was where we decided to avail ourselves of all remaining innocence before the end. We already kept so many secrets there.

"If planes and satellites are going to fall out of the sky," Crystal said, entertaining just for a moment the silly notion that a computer glitch would steal her fate. "I refuse to die a fucking virgin."

Thirty minutes before midnight, I declined a call from my mom at the Vista jail and let Crystal's dad pour the remainder of a handle of Cuervo into my plastic cup. "To be so goddamn young again," he whispered, not to me, but to the sea.

We would learn a lot about the world that didn't end. Like how Crystal's hymen wouldn't break, couldn't break, not without twilight anesthesia. Or how alcohol made Jimmy have seizures and AC/DC gave Janae orgasms. We would learn how Rob took his dad's rifle down to Tamarack Beach, alone, fully loaded. That existential dread was just one more inch of shadow. The cameras at the vet where I bagged dead animals and sterilized scalpels were just dummies—they never caught me slipping vials of ketamine into my scrub pants. They never caught me crying over my mother's voicemails.

Midnight came and went.

Earl shotgunned a beer.

Kelsey swallowed a pill.

Kemp sucked down a can of air duster and plowed his Mitsubishi through the lowered arm of Pendleton's D Gate.

Crystal's Dad handed me a cigarette. And then reached for the moon.

"Time is a shrinking knot," he said, crying. "We have to cut our own ends."

The sun stretched its neck as it rose over the silent cul de sac. It reached into the sidewalk cracks and swept through the tired palms.

I stood at the threshold of driveway and asphalt, dumbfounded. I didn't know where to begin again.

It wouldn't take us long to learn that the world doesn't care about prophecies or numbers or our endless methods of self-destruction. The world—thank God—is incapable of making any promise we expect it to keep.

Undertow

We pinned their name tags to our knitted sacks. Reynolds. Solomon. Childs. Kennedy. We wrote their room numbers on our wrists and waited for them on the cement benches near the Commandant's office. We sat with our legs crossed, lanyards between our fingers, condoms in our hip pockets.

They marched the line in their parade uniforms.

We tracked sand from dorm to bedroom sheets. Our mothers washed their civvies and kept them in the guest room or the pool house, convinced we were the ones doing the civilizing.

There were boys whose names we couldn't share. Boys whose names we'd seen taped inside other girls' lockers. Boys whose hips were like rip tides. Boys with thirsty eyes. Boys in beach stairwells and stolen cars. Boys in bathroom stalls above the fire pits at Coyote, behind the air hockey tables in Mr. Peabody's.

Wharton. Claussen. Holt. Phelps.

We carried their desire. We carried the sea.

When they were expelled or graduated or disappeared, we framed their names with the Christmas lights on our bulletin boards. We cocooned ourselves in our salty-air bedrooms and drank wine coolers and collaged, high on unspent touch, sweating them out like a forever hangover. Eschholz, Brady, Coy. We kept their parents' secrets and sent encrypted letters. Silently thanked God for cigarettes and earthquakes and all things California.

It is November and my children are on their way home from school. I've been thinking about the tapes, where I put them, who is on them. I write the names on a legal pad with my stick figure portrait and a long-past pediatrician appointment scribbled in the corner. Heinneman. Daltz. Prescott. Gregory. The spellings don't look right. I dig through a box harboring those fugitive years. I don't find the tapes, but I find photos that are too blurry for confirmation.

I read an article about the Commandant who gave whiskey to the boys and took them home. It explains nothing and recalls everything. The cadet who drowned in the undertow by the academy barracks. The dime bags he kept in his beret. The upperclassman who would fuck me so long as I didn't touch him back, his moaning in the beach stairwell, my fingers blistering on the chain-link fence, his blank unrecognition when I saw him at the winter formal. There was the freshman from Texas who sold pills. The Chaplain's son who bought and could not stop taking the pills. The junior officer who drank a handle of Popov and told us what had been done to him. The boy who slept with his rifle. The boy who fucked his rifle. The marksman who wrote poems and was sent to the desert. Somewhere in between, sometime after, there was the one who called to tell me he'd been released from San Quentin, to say he is not a boy anymore.

The Commandant's face is waxy like honeydew. His name, common as salt.

The boys' names have been redacted—McKee and Smith and Wright—but I hear them—Webb and Fritz and Oh—calling from the Mariana Trench, whispering just below the surface, translating the language of sand far from the sea.

2001: Notes

That was the last of the endless summers. The summer before El Nino. The summer of rip tides and night swimming.

We left enough sand on the Tacoma's floorboards to build a skyscraper. Soaked the driver's seat with salt. Josh played the *Singles* soundtrack while I sucked the heat off of an entire bag of fireballs. I should have recognized it then, but I didn't. I thought pain was the touchstone of desire. But love can be a gesture, a touch so gentle it doesn't leave marks.

That was the summer Joe gave up being an anarchist and enlisted in the Army. They gave him $50,000 in life insurance and a service pistol and shipped him away on the 12th of September.

That was the summer we chased ghosts in Elfin Forest and got blacklisted from Motel 6. When we fell in love with New Radicals and Radiohead. That was the summer all those last-call tourists were hit by Amtraks near Boar's Crossing, when we chain-smoked Camel Red Lights in Nikki's garage and plucked our eyebrows into oblivion.

Because the adult world was obscene and cold, we learned every obscenity and drew ourselves to every fire. We treated our CD cases like safety deposit boxes and our bodies like experiments. Everyone was fucking everyone that summer. Except the boys who lived in Yellow House—the girls who saved themselves for the lip of a perfect wave.

That was the summer Dad broke down bedroom doors, the summer I held dogs and cats as they were euthanized, wheeling their still-warm bodies in black trash bags to the basement freezer for D&D pick-up. That was the summer Anita started fucking Dr. Saldarriaga in his La Jolla townhouse and I fainted in the breakroom, anemic after they burned the cancer from my seventeen-year-old cervix.

That was the last of the endless summers.

I served Thanksgiving dinner at the VA where Mom was getting sober that fall, and with the money from my job at the vet, I bought the Sony Hi-8 that would take me, desperate and half-alive, to the film school that made Zemeckis and rejected Spielberg, that bore Lucas's name on nearly every building. At the end of November, before I ran away, I used the screen to tell our secrets. We drank what was in the bottles, procured real needles, kissed each other raw. Because we loved Tarantino and Scorsese but wanted to be brut like Solondz and Clark—we didn't know any better—we cast our real-life entourages and taped our fragile devastations. We faked cocaine deaths to "Lucky Man" by The Verve and watched, without a fuck to give, as our hearts exploded inside of the Proscenium. Mr. Beauvais called it genius, and I think Jackie's parents called CPS.

No one talked about the fires. We didn't think much of them then. We were trying to stay alive, walking the edge of the razor. We were too focused on the drop below.

Forever franchises fell like dominoes that year. There would be no more Friday nights at Sizzler, no more stealing crystals from Natural Wonders. That was the year they started locking the food in their bedroom. The year we stopped having dinner at all.

I buy too much food now, and when it goes bad, I cry.

They say you can feel a sea change, that you can pinpoint the moment zeitgeist slips away. Twenty years later, I'm still holding the photos, rewinding the tapes, and unfolding the origamied testimonies. I'm still trying to feel that feeling—so that I can let it go.

TAPE #3: 9/12/01

INT. WARNER MEDIA STUDIO - OFFLINE EDITING
BAY - DAY

An elite private editing suite with
ergonomic chairs, ambient track lighting,
black foam acoustic panels, Dolby Atmos
surround. This is the Don Perignon of
editing bays.

Paled by the light of three 27" editing
monitors, AMBER FOLEY, 36, sits at the
helm, arms folded across her chest. She's
a late Gen-X mom of two, rocking business
casual with a "Ceci n'est pas une pipe"
shirt and boyfriend blazer. This is not
her first time in a state-of-the-art
studio, but her caution might be
misinterpreted as nerves.

Sporting gold-rimmed Windsors and head-
to-toe black, PETER SANDBERG, 62, grizzled
with more salt than pepper, watches the
PLAYBACK MONITOR over Amber's shoulder.
He's hovering like a sweat bee. Always TOO
CLOSE.

ON THE PLAYBACK MONITOR

Grainy footage of an early 2000s house
party. Out-of-focus faces and bodies wipe
the foreground. Blur screen left. Cut
screen right. Eventually, bare shoulders
and bottles and cigarette smoke part to
reveal the focus of the HANDHELD shot -

A tall, pale drink of water in a NoFX shirt
and (if we could see them) newly purchased

combat boots, leaning against the graffitied living room wall. Frameless glasses, soft jaw, and fresh high and tight, he's barely the legal drinking age but knows his way around a bar. This is JOE.

To the right of Joe, a stolen metal security sign is screwed into the wall:

"SMILE YOU ARE ON CAMERA"

Realizing he's being watched, Joe turns his attention to US. He looks INTO THE CAMERA, flips us off, then makes a gun. He aims, and then fires. We are not deterred. He blows imaginary smoke from the barrel and takes a sip of beer from a bottle with the label ripped off.

BACK TO SCENE

Peter rubs his unshaven chin. Setttles back into the swivel chair.

> PETER
> We're going to have to send a second unit down to film some B-roll and establishing shots. You've got too many close-ups in this footage. I'm claustrophobic.

> AMBER
> I was sixteen. I was in my early Tarantino phase. Every person was like Butch Coolidge to me. I was always trying to catch the eye light and hold on

as long as I could.

                    PETER
          God, if only you could zoom
          out.

                    AMBER
          We both know that's not how
          tape works.

                    PETER
          Neither does RAW.

                    AMBER
          No, but with RAW you can at
          least set a wide shot and punch
          in without losing resolution.
          You don't have to think about
          frame perimeter anymore. You
          just point, shoot, fix in post.
          Technology does all of the
          work.

                    PETER
          There's a lot of movement. I
          don't remember the Tribeca
          short being so bouncy. It won't
          be as bad screening on a phone,
          but holy shit, we're going to
          have to hand out Dramamine and
          Vicodin at the DGA premiere.

Amber takes a deep breath. Tries to let
"DGA" and all of the baggage packed into
those three letters roll off of her back.

                    AMBER
          I was still learning how to
          steady my handhelds. Also,

those early aughts Sonys had zero stabilization.

She clicks a file in the media bin, types something into the metadata box, and moves on to the next clip.

It becomes clear that they have been at this for hours.

ON THE PLAYBACK MONITOR

The CAMERA ZOOMS OUT to reveal a small living room full of surfer-punks and stoners in their late teens and early 20s. Bottles and ashtrays and Big Gulps clutter the coffee table, where a few shirtless, tattooed guys in cargo shorts and backwards baseball caps play Grand Theft Auto.

                PETER (O.S.)
     There we go.

As the CAMERA SCANS the room, we get a snapshot of the best and worst of turn-of-the-millennium SoCal fashion. Everyone is smoking. Everyone is drinking. Everyone is talking over everyone else and moving through the room as if they have some place else to go. But no one seems to leave.

This is YELLOW HOUSE.

BACK TO SCENE
Peter leans into Amber again, reaches over her shoulder to point at the monitor.

                    PETER
Who's the fag holding the Zippo
with the anarchy symbol?

               AMBER
     (softly)
That's JP.

                    PETER
I don't remember him from the
short either. He's a good-
looking kid.

               AMBER
He was.
     (then)
I don't think many of us felt
like kids. I wish I could
remember when I stopped
feeling like a kid.

               PETER
What happened to him? Did he
turn into a jarhead like what's
his name?

               AMBER
Joe.

               PETER
Yeah, Joe.

               AMBER
No. And Joe was a soldier, not
a marine. JP couldn't join the
Army, not that he wanted to.
His seizure disorder made him
ineligible.

Peter sits back in his chair, running both hands through his grizzle.

                    PETER
          Eh, he's too pretty for war
          anyway. Those towelheads would
          have eaten him alive.

                    AMBER
          JP knew bokator. He almost
          killed a Suey for spitting on
          his longboard once.

                    PETER
          What's a Suey?

                    AMBER
          A Suicidal. They were an
          Oceanside gang we sometimes
          clashed with.

                    PETER
          Oh, shit. You all were
          gangbangers? How come that
          didn't make it into the Tribeca
          short?

                    AMBER
          We weren't gangbangers.

                    PETER
          ...whoa...hold on, hold on.
          What's that?

                    AMBER
          What's what?

                    PETER
          Go to the head of that last
          clip.

We stay on AMBER as Peter pushes in,
pressing his chest against her shoulder.
She taps a few hot keys to maneuver the
playhead and then uses the mouse to switch
monitor views.

                    AMBER
          Where? Here?

                    PETER
          No...

Reaching from behind, Peter places his
HAND over Amber's on the MOUSE. We remain
in CLOSEUP as he drags her hand and the
mouse across the tracking pad.

                    PETER (CONT'D)
               (softly)
          ...here.

                                   CUT TO:

PETER'S MOUTH

hardly a centimeter from Amber's ear.

                    PETER (CONT'D)
          That.

BACK TO SCENE

He STRIKES the spacebar and leans back
into his chair. Amber takes a moment,
studies the screen.

                    PETER (CONT'D)
          That's Joe, right?

                         AMBER
          Yeah.

                         PETER
          Look at the mirror.

                         AMBER
          Mirror?

                         PETER
          Right third. Behind the girl
          with the bomber jacket.

                         AMBER
          Oh, my god.

                         PETER
          I don't know how you did it,
          but that's a pretty good camera
          trick.

                         AMBER
          I didn't do anything. He
          doesn't have a reflection.

                         PETER
          It doesn't even look like an
          optical illusion.

          Amber moves the playback head to the
          beginning of the CLIP. Her finger hovers
          above the spacebar.

                         AMBER
                    (softly)
          He was dead already.

TAPE #21: 5/17/05

Offline Assistant Editor Meeting

[Transcript]

How did Danny start the fire?
He used gasoline from the 76 station across the street, the one by the Motel 6 where we used to pay cash for rooms the year before the towers fell and Joe went off to Iraq. When I asked him later, Danny said he started with the bedroom carpet but became less deliberate as he went along.

What did you say when he told you that?
I said, "And you filmed it? With *my* camera?"

And what did he say?
He said, "Hell yeah, I filmed it. Wouldn't you?"

Did you think that was weird?
Of course I thought it was weird. But then I watched the tapes. Not just his and not just the fire. I watched mine, too, the ones from before Joe left.

What were you filming?
I wasn't sure at the time. Everyone. Everything. All I knew was that the towers were there and then they weren't, and thousands of people were dead and nothing was ever going to be the same. I knew Joe was going away. I didn't know if he was coming back.

*

What did Danny burn?
The past.

Whose past?
Joe's. Mine. Anybody's.

What else did he burn?
He wouldn't say.

What is the temperature of fire?
Depends on the ignition source, the accelerant. The house burned at a cool 1,900°F.

At what temperature does steel melt?
2,500°F. Sometimes hotter.

And the towers?
They more than burned.

How do you know all of this?
I read a lot of stuff. On the internet.

You can find anything on the internet.
Yeah, you can. That's why everyone's so scared all of the time now.

*

Where was Joe during all of this?
In the bathtub.

Why was he taking a bath?

He wasn't.

Did Danny know he was in the house?
Danny did what he was told to do.

Who told him to light the fire?
Joe did.

*

I'm confused. If Joe was in the bathtub—
He was. And then he wasn't. Here, watch the tape.

Is he wearing—?
Fatigues, yeah. Just watch. At the seven-minute mark, you'll see it. You'll see the flashover and then—

Holy shit.
Right?

Incinerated.
Nope.

What do you mean?
He didn't burn. They didn't find him anywhere. There was *nothing*. No bones, no bullet.

Bullet?
Joe took a bullet through the back in Fallujah. It was so close to his spine that they left it in.

At what temperature does a bullet melt?
300ish.

Then it could have been there.
Right. But it wouldn't evaporate. It would deform. They would have found the puddle of it when they cleared the tub. And Joe, of course.

What the—
It's crazy shit, huh? Do you want to watch it again? At quarter-speed?

*

What happened to Danny?
Nothing at first. No one had wanted the house there for as long as anyone could remember, but Danny held on to it through the years. It was his and Joe's. Things had been built up around it—the motel, the gas station, another motel, the Circle K. There were no neighbors, no other damaged structures. Because no one filed an insurance claim, the initial arson investigations were abandoned. After it burned, Danny sold the land quickly, to a developer who eventually turned it into a self-storage facility.

*

What did Danny do with the money from the land?
He went off to film school like I did. Got sober like a lot of us did. Got medicated and talked back to sanity, or something close. He bought a small cement marker in an underwater cemetery on the north side of Catalina Island and put Joe's name on it, despite Joe's wishes to be forgotten.

But I thought you said they never found the body.

They didn't.

You don't mark graves for people who are still alive. Unless you are trying to hide something.
Joe died long before Danny set the fire.

*

What happened to Danny in the end?
There is no end. He's still kicking. He's making recruiting videos now for the marines over at Camp Pendleton. He's saving up to buy another house. He's paying off his student loans. He's contemplating buying life insurance even though he has no beneficiaries…but they don't care about that. They only care about the fire. That's all they want to see, you know. They forget that a fire leaves ashes behind. They don't really understand.

Who are "they"?
The network. The studio. The producers who think they know what this story is about but don't have a fucking clue. *They* never do.

Why didn't they ask Danny to make this film?
I'm the one with the tapes. I'm the one who kept the proof all this time.

Since "they" don't know the story, why don't you show me? Like this shot here. What's the real story behind it?
That's where I'm struggling. Tape has limitations. It only captures what can be seen: two young guys in white T-shirts and black baseball caps standing side-by-side. Two friends casually disinterested in the room, the people, the

world. On tape, the moment is a blip. A tattooed hand on the nape of a bare neck. A softening jaw. But there's more than the tape shows. If you'd have been there, you'd know what I mean. You'd have felt their bodies refusing to be bodies anymore. You'd have understood. They were going to have to become one shape if they were going to be able to hold it all in. Time, touch, urgency, and the thing under the thing that we could all see back then but chose not to. The thing we were too afraid to see because the world told us we could only be afraid.

Which was what?
Love.

TAPE #6: 10/27/01

INT. WARNER MEDIA COMMISSARY - DAY

A little too late for lunch. A little too
early for dinner. Peter and Amber sit in
the bright, open-air cafeteria near a wall
of iron menagerie-style windows. Amber
sips a Diet Coke and picks at an
overflowing basket of seasoned curly
fries. Peter eats a frozen lemonade with
a spoon throughout.

One might assume they are the only people
on Earth. Or that this film could not
afford the atmosphere. Or that Peter has
orchestrated this isolation. This
constant privacy.

                    PETER
           (spooning his lemonade)
        How bad did it get?

                    AMBER
        Really bad.

                    PETER
        Did you kill anyone?

                    AMBER
        No.

                    PETER
        Did you total your car?

                    AMBER
        No.

                    PETER
          Did you get a DUI?

                         AMBER
          No.

                    PETER
          Did you lose your house or your
          husband or your kids?

                         AMBER
          No. Not yet.

Amber shoves three curly fries into her
mouth and watches as GEORGE CLOONEY,
smoking a cigarette and dressed in a
steampunk tuxedo, rides past the
commissary window on a GOLF CART driven by
a stone-faced PA.

                    PETER
          So what happened?

                         AMBER
          Nothing.

                    PETER
          Nothing?

Amber watches Peter suck juice out of the
iced lemonade. He sets it down, leaving
the ice.

                    PETER
          If nothing happened, how could
          it have been that bad?

                    AMBER
It's a nightmare to miss out on
your own life.
        (then)
And I was missing everything.

Agua Hedionda

The townhouse on Agua Hedionda is two miles from the payphone on PCH where Janae picks me up, but it's too early for Bob to be awake and we are too sober to head over, so we have a few shots of Malibu in the parking lot of Pig Liquor and cruise north to The Strand Bar where we can bum smokes while Janae presses her perfect tits up against Will.

It's 2pm on a Thursday, the middle of an Indian summer, and there are no empty bar stools. A marine with a Semper Fi tat on his left calf buys me two Jäger bombs and traces cinch knots on the small of my back. I like watching him watch me eye the man with the black pool cue assuming the shooting position between pockets. I like smoking his Parliaments. Two months from now, when Janae disappears, I won't remember names. I'll only remember how he sunk a stripe on the break, where his teeth singed my neck like frozen glass.

I'm drifting towards the sea of baize when Janae says she got a text from Bob. We peace out, leave the marine and Will—hot, tight, and eager—behind the bar. We throw a few winks at the palisade of dark-eyed men watching us from behind bottomless drinks.

In the car, Janae hits the bottle of Malibu, hands it to me.

"Don't worry," she says, plunging the key into the ignition. "Bob's chill as fuck."

All I know about Bob is he's forty-two, likes to party, and owns a Maaco in Anaheim. Janae's not sleeping with him. She's not sleeping with anyone. But like every man who meets her, he loves to have her around, to keep the idea of her close, to wish upon her body like a star.

Bob's front door is open when we arrive. I'm two inches taller than the man with veneers who hands us Coronas and introduces the person reclining on his couch as Deuce, the roommate. Janae's face tells me this is a new development, and I'm not sure why it should matter except that Deuce is clammy and unshaven, sporting combat boots with cutoff jeans and a high and tight that is overgrown. I peg him for a jarhead right away, assume he's AWOL from Pendleton or worse.

While Bob and Janae do lines in the kitchen, Deuce shuffles out of the room. He returns after a few minutes, holding a shoebox. The lights dim as he lowers himself next to me, chewing the filter on his Newport. He talks to me without talking to me. He tells me how Bob got a new water heater last Tuesday, how he caught two halibut in Agua Hedionda that tasted like sulfur. He tells me how the Marines raped him of his manhood, how he hasn't fucked anyone in over a year.

He slides the box into the middle of the coffee table.

He tells me how heavy a dead child is.

"Once they're stiff," he says, chewing, smoking, "their ears peel off like oranges."

He removes the lid from the shoebox. It's full of pictures.

After Janae disappears, they'll drag Agua Hedionda for two days. They'll ask whether I've been to Bob's Maaco or know a man named John. I'll wonder how they came up with their questions, whether they knew what I'd done with the marine at the bar.

"What the fuck, Bob?" Janae is standing behind me, pointing down with her cigarette.

The rain sprays like bullets through the patio light

outside of the open sliding glass door. I can smell the lagoon's rotting kelp.

Bob enters from the kitchen all eyes and mouth and wildness. He hands me the rolled bill and a resin tray and tugs the chest hair fighting his Tommy Bahama.

"They aren't real," he says. Then, to Deuce, "What the fuck did I tell you about those pictures?"

Deuce apologizes to the floor. He closes the box and shuffles down the unlit hallway, returns empty-handed, slouching and smoking by the open sliding door. I pause, make sure he isn't watching me, and then do a line.

Someone is blasting Marvin Gaye's "Got to Give It Up" across the lagoon, and Janae is fighting Bob for the keys to his boat. Deuce studies the dirt under his fingernails, sweat clustering between his eyebrows. He mumbles something about showers and skinny dipping, and I'm thinking of telling him how I almost drowned last week because of the rip tides, how the warm water from El Niño kills off tens of thousands of fish and seals every cycle. But Janae is yelling now and someone is laughing and I'm being sucked out the drain of a door and into the passenger seat. Outside, it isn't raining, but the windshield is wet, and the asphalt shimmers like an upside-down pool beneath the streetlights.

"It's night," I say. My hands are rubber dumbbells.

Janae doesn't have power steering, but she muscles the car onto Tamarack without much effort, putting Agua Hedionda and Bob's townhouse behind us.

"Next time, we'll take the boat out," she says. "Fucking tweakers."

We cruise north on the PCH again, pass the bowling alley, the garish fluorescent glow from the military depot. Janae puts Nelly Furtado in the disc changer and drapes her bangled wrist out the window where the ocean is a black eel keeping an easy pace.

After they find Janae's body, they'll stop asking questions and I'll start having nightmares. Children tangled in seaweed. Seals buried in the Arabian desert. I'll constantly be on the verge of asking why terrible things only happen to some people.

Before we get out of the car, Janae leans over and kisses me. She smells like Tova and rum.

We step out into a sudden gust of Santa Anas. When you live by the beach, night is its own season. Beyond the small parking lot, the empty beach is pale and waiting beneath the breaking waves.

I follow Janae down a set of concrete steps through the back door of The Strand Bar, snake with her through the smoke and light, around the crowded high tops.

I'm center frame, the subject of a moving beauty shot.

And I'm not thinking about Deuce or Bob or shoeboxes or oranges. I'm not thinking about the undertow or the tide or the lagoon's filthy water. I'm done with thinking. I'm focusing on feeling, enjoying the body heat. I'm scanning the room. Deciding how I want to move through it, how to make it feel good. I'm anticipating the man with the pool cue. Where it will happen. What his mouth will taste like. What songs I want to play for him on the jukebox and where I will draw the line. I'm thinking about how the night is young and I'm full of possibilities—a burning star.

Check Your Risk Level

Shoshona got her period the day after the Fallbrook Fire erupted east of Highway 15 and incinerated hundreds of acres of pot and palm tree farms. Her boyfriend blamed blue balls. Her nana blamed MTV. Us? We knew better than to point fingers.

We knew there were other ways to start fires.

"I'm so sick of this shithole," Kelsey told me over a carne asada burrito in the hotel beach access. It was Good Friday. The air was still cottony with weed smoke and palm ash. We should've been in AP Chemistry, but Kelsey's parents were at a Harley show in Reno, so we got stoned in Kelsey's bedroom and spent the morning making out. The beach access was our shared version of limbo. We would sit fifty feet up from the sand, claim the cement landing between three stories of multi-million-dollar luxury real estate as ours—and scowl at the narrow frame of sea below.

"I wonder what it was like," I said, "to not be afraid of water."

Kelsey dug a piece of charred meat out of her teeth and flicked it towards the waves. "After graduation," she said, "I'm moving to New York."

"What's in New York?"

"Cement. Steel. Fire departments," Kelsey winked at me through a triumph of red curls, "and *real* lesbians."

We both knew everything burned. We'd come of age in endless smoke. We'd survived on desert shorelines and learned to extinguish our bodies in the Pacific. The sea, they said, would asphyxiate what was programmed to combust. So when our brothers and boyfriends and parents grew fearful, they sent us west, sent us to water, demanded we submerge, stay under until the North Pacific gyre had made us sufficiently numb.

They called it curing girls for fire season. But we knew that was bullshit. They were trying to do so much more than douse our phantom fires before they started. They were trying to extinguish the light at the source, to prevent it from shining at all.

Some of us took matters into our own hands. We knew the droughts would keep coming, that we would be blamed for the fires, that there was a reason we'd be given nothing to protect ourselves.

Emily survived the Elfin Forest Fire by creating a controlled burn beside her grandma's jacuzzi. She used Asa's love letters and the bottle of Popov her brother Joe left under the bed when he deployed.

They used to send us away from May to August. To church camp, to grandparents' houses in the sticks.

That's all changed now that the world is dying and fire season never ends. Summer is longer—and not in the ways we wanted it to be.

There were millions of dumb ways adults tried to "cure girls for fire season." For whatever reason, most started with a home remodel or relandscaping.

Ilene's dad was first to install tile floors and buy flame resistant sheets, but Nikki's mom was the first to talk to us about the real risks of nights, all their unspent heat and desire—"the time of greatest flammability."

"Fourteen. That's when I started using metal cases for my cigarettes," she said, taking a long drag on her Capri. She was trying to caution us, to comfort us with her experience. But I couldn't take my eyes off of her fresh acrylics, the way they reflected the light of the sun like tiny mirrors.

The summer before I started high school, I got breasts and three smoking tickets from the same beach cop on bike. Dad razed the ice plant and honeysuckle and installed a fence-to-fence pool and granite patio. It was like the fucking Parthenon.

"I got this system," Dad said, gesturing towards his $50,000 investment. "If a teenage boy's penis so much as *skims* the top of that pool, the water will turn blood red—and I'm going to *know*."

Our parents didn't understand. They thought we avoided the pools because we were focused on our tans. It didn't matter that California was in a drought and had been for fifty years. For my parents, the cost of curing was not even a question.

Lydia pierced her bellybutton the summer we lost our virginity. She fell asleep on the beach while listening to Patti Smith and woke up with a constellation of glass in her stomach. The barbell looked like a fresh railroad tie. To be fair, the Santa Anas had been blowing all week, so it was only a matter of time before one of us got too hot for too long and melted a thing or two.

"Lydia, who've you been dickin' around with?" Anita whispered. We were huddled in the corner of an air-conditioned waiting room full of construction workers and a boy who'd shoved a Lego up his nose.

"No one!" Lydia wept. "Not since Brian." Then, "Do you think it'll scar?"

"Those Yellow House boys are sketch," I said, uneasy. I still hadn't told her about the sleeping bag and the Underground and how I'd hooked up with Brian two weeks before she'd hooked up with him at Beth's Motel 6 party. It didn't bother me the way I knew it would bother her. I liked Brian, but I liked a lot of people. Girls. Boys. People. And anyway, fucking Brian hadn't been about fucking Brian. It had been about seeing the forest for the trees. *And it felt good. Everywhere.* But, still. I wondered. *Will I be next?* Would I have to atone for pleasure? Would I wake up to see my mother's jacaranda burned to the ground? Would I succumb to shame and shrapnel like Lydia or Aubrey or Dani or Natasha?

Any girl can start a grassfire with her bare knees. They told us that from an early age: Keep your skirts long and your shoulders bloused. Before you leave for school, check your risk level. Raise your arms above your head and squat down onto your haunches. Is your ass showing? Can you see your hip flexors? Think about where you fall on the danger scale. If it's a Red Flag Warning kind of day, call the school and tell them to send your work home. If it's prom week, know where your portable extinguisher is. I kept an E-Jet aerosol in the water bottle pocket of my Jansport that Mom bought from Duluth or Bartact when they had sales, usually around Easter or Memorial Day.

To be honest?

I'd never seen a girl start a fire.

But I'd felt the blistering heat of a lie. All of us had.

The last summer they sent me away to my aunt's house in Humboldt, everything changed. While my aunt and uncle were off playing disc golf with friends from their local mycological society, I smoked an unfinished joint I found in one of the ashtrays and stumbled across a slim book, "Against Curing Girls for Fire Season," tucked between two vegan cookbooks in the pantry. It didn't have an ISBN number or a publisher or copyright year, but the paper felt like silk between my fingers.

I snuck it home in my college applications Pee Chee, and when I wasn't wearing the sheen down on its glossy pages, I hid it in the Thriller vinyl tacked to my bedroom wall.

Sometime in November, I think it was right after the Valley Fire wiped out the last of Escondido's vineyards, Kelsey accepted a full ride to NYU for their music industry program. I was still waiting to hear back from a handful of film schools, all west of the Mississippi.

"What if it's the same there?" I asked her. "I heard there are sharks in the East River."

"Pink dolphins, too," Kelsey smiled, leaning away from me, into the beach access railing. "You can't get any gayer than that."

I read the book to Anita and Kelsey in the Taco Bell parking lot while we waited for AJ to pick us up and take us to Yellow House.

"'...all this talk of catastrophe and fearmongering,'"—it was my favorite part—"'is willful baptism by fire. We cannot let fear silence us like smoke. Fear itself is the accelerant.'"

Kelsey lit a cigarette, listened with the intensity of a barracuda. "'...we must stop them from proselytizing our bodies. We must teach each other how to recover from these lies. We must show each other how to rise from the ashes of our oppressors and live anew.'"

The words ricocheted off the parking pylons, into the afternoon traffic. Anita passed me her horchata and stood up. Her eyes glistened. She was awake.

"Here," I placed the pamphlet in her outstretched hand. "What do you think?"

"I think..." she started, watching AJ's white Seabreeze pull into the parking lot, "things aren't going to be the same anymore. They can't be."

Spencer opened the passenger door and gestured at his crotch, "There's room on my lap for a hottie."

"You wish, Spoons," Anita said, eyes glued to a page I'd marked in red.

AJ, motionless behind the wheel, fist-bumped me through the driver's side window as I sardined myself onto the split-leathered back seat. Anita rode bitch, her face pushed deep into the book's loosening binding. I could feel my heart racing to catch up with the excitement of this secret I'd discovered and released into the world. I had no idea what we would do with it. All I knew was that everything had changed, and I didn't want it to go back to the way it was.

Halfway to Yellow House, Kelsey unbuckled her seatbelt. She tossed her half-smoked cigarette out the window.

"Come here," she whispered, reaching, swimming across the fishnet landscape of Anita's lap until she arrived at the horizon of my body, until she crested me like a rising sun and everything was touch and light and so hard, so hot, I couldn't tell who was melting who—I didn't care—all I knew was that we'd never let them force us underwater again.

TAPE #9: 2/12/02

INT. WARNER MEDIA STUDIO – OFFLINE EDITING
BAY – DAY

Peter and Amber sit across from each
other. Amber's back is to the editing
monitors. A RENDERING progress bar shows
50% completion.

Peter pulls a metal cigarette case out of
his jacket pocket. He removes a clove and
lights the end of it with a butane
lighter. He inhales, causing the cigarette
to CRACKLE.

> AMBER
> We used to say that's the sound
> of your lungs bleeding.

> PETER
> Oh, yeah? Well, don't tell my
> pulmonologist.
>> (then)
> You want one?

> AMBER
> I do.
>> (she waves him away)
> But I can't.

Peter puts the lighter away and nods
towards the monitor.

> PETER
> How much time do we have?

                    AMBER
It's almost done. Our meeting
wasn't supposed to be until two
o'clock --

                    PETER
And I just couldn't wait.

                    AMBER
--so it's going to be a minute.
     (then)
It's good. I mean, *I* think it
is.

                    PETER
The Tribeca short --

                    AMBER
"They More Than Burned."

                    PETER
--that   was...*intimate*.   You
were... a *witness*. The camera
was *your eye*. Seeing this new
bit of raw footage and knowing
some of what else you've got in
those   other   tapes...I   think
there's a lot of room to open
up. I think you can create more
space and let the audience in.
Even with all these fucking
close-ups.

                    AMBER
Okay.

                    PETER
We'll get new interviews. Some
"where they are twenty years

after the attack" footage.

          AMBER
That's going to be really hard
to do.

          PETER
You have to trust the process,
okay. Be open to feedback.
You're not editing a twenty-
minute short in your bedroom
anymore. You're creating a
major network feature
documentary.

          AMBER
I understand. And I am
appreciative. It's just that
it's going to be really hard to
conduct new interviews.

          PETER
You're not alone anymore.
We've got resources. We'll
track everyone down. We'll do
the reaching out and the
scheduling and the deal memos.
That's why we're here. You
don't have to worry about that
shit anymore. That's off your
plate.

          AMBER
I appreciate that, but there's
a bigger issue.

Peter pulls on the clove. CRACKLE.

                    PETER
              (exhaling)
And what's that?

                    AMBER
Almost everyone on these tapes
is dead.

                    PETER
And yet you're still here.

                    AMBER
That's right. I am.

NINE BODIES I DIDN'T LEAVE BEHIND

THE SOPHOMORE IN THE PLAY

The body in the cement sidewalk is mine. He told several people he was going to do it, that he'd been planning it since he took me to homecoming and I refused to kiss him on my father's doorstep. The sequence of him chasing me with a sonnet in the dark was a horror I concealed with white out and Zima and a steady rotation of Dispatch and The Doors. If only I'd been at the coffeeshop to answer the payphone when Mary called between dress rehearsals; if only I'd allowed him touch -- some greater sympathy for his alienation, that solitude I'd convinced myself belonged to Lawrence's disgraced Bertram Cates -- there would have been no blood spatter on stage right, no trail of evidence leading to a carport in Encinitas, to the foundation that never had enough time to dry. If I'd been there to answer the payphone when Mary called, I'd have called 911, I'd have hidden in the bathroom while they confiscated the Mossberg 500 in his locker and escorted him through campus in cuffs. I'd have gone home and contemplated the bottom of my father's pool, convinced I was a soft weapon and it had all been my fault.

THE CO-ED IN THE ATTIC

The body in the attic is mine. The boys won't say whom the necktie belonged to, even though everyone had seen Brad tracking me through the party. At what point does loneliness become a weapon? If it ever comes out, if the swabs come back dirty, the boys will say it was a game. Brad was a stray. He wasn't theirs. Wasn't even a student at the college -- wasn't more than a ghost trapped behind the bookshelf under the staircase when Los Angeles got too dry, too dirty, too lonely to sustain him.

THE AMERICAN IN THE RIVER

The body in the Vltava is mine. It was never supposed to float. The man with the mattress in his basement window was last seen getting on the metro in Anděl, heading towards Černý Most and its impenetrable palisade of paneláks. You saw him, too. Refilling my wine glass all night at U Sudu and feigning sips of his Beton. The PČR mistake me for an ice floe at first, but my face is no longer concealed by the mottled bedsheet, and the diamond earrings my grandfather gifted me when I was twelve sparkle below the lights of Národní Divadlo, direct them to my chrysalis frozen in the eddy. Andromeda winking at me.

THE HOSTAGE ON THE PLANE

One of the bodies in the Bally's penthouse is mine. It takes the investigators two days to get half of the story from Nadine and only after she's been released on $1,000 bail from Clark County Detention Center. No one knew the Australian's real name, she told them. One minute I was shooting pool at Lucy's, the next, I was two eight balls high on a flight to Vegas with not so much as a toothbrush for my stay. Nadine doesn't remember the Australian's name or why he insisted on buying the tickets. His hands, she says. Her neck, she says. My name, she says, over and over, like a bird in broken song.

THE YOUNG ASSISTANT IN THE HEADLINES

The body in the cassette room is mine. Ernie has been planning to fuck me since the first day I brought him coffee on set, but he never knew what he really wanted until he had me pinned against his front door. I should be on Stage 23 at the studio lot right now, watching pre-shoots from video village, a final draft of the 98th episode in one hand and two sharpened pencils for Cohen and Forester in the other. If he hadn't broken his foot, if I hadn't brought him those Vicodin like he'd asked me to, if the showrunner hadn't told me to drive him home so he could get his shit together...it was supposed to be a tour and then done: the tape room, the vinyl room, the cassette room, the room where he and Bob recorded Theme Time Radio Hour--

--I was supposed to be pliant. I was supposed to be grateful.

THE MOTHER IN THE ROAD

The body in the road is mine. The driver of the car doesn't know my name or where I live. He doesn't remember me telling him my husband will divorce me and take the kids. He doesn't remember what drinks he bought me, which pill he slipped me, or whether he paid the tab. He only remembers my devastation when Neil Young sang "Cowgirl in the Sand," the soft halo of my black hair. Anger is a fault line under pressure. He only remembers pressure. How it felt to shake the earth with his desire, to see the mountain of me collapse.

THE MOTHER IN THE DITCH

The body in the ditch is mine. Our two other children are home waiting. You are home waiting, watching for my texts, uneasy about me being alone in the clinic 45 miles past the state line where I don't have to consult a psychologist first or speak to a member of the clergy -- where the $400 we scraped together would prevent what the broken condom couldn't. I don't tell you what the clinicians say after three hours of waiting in triage, that taking the Mifepristone means I would have to stop nursing our son, that the surgical alternative was the same price, that women who had given birth before tolerated the vacuum just fine. All it takes is the threat of a broken heart and ten minutes of a doctor with bullet hole scars in his arms narrating the MLB draft to me over the sound of suction. All it takes is thinking of my sweet boy waiting at home, hungry, wanting nothing but my skin and milk dreams.

(a beat)

The ditch I'm in is three miles from home. Blood hemorrhages through the driver's seat of the 4-Runner I abandoned on the shoulder ten yards away. When the tow truck comes, you will find our family Christmas photo stuck to a dark patch of asphalt near the front tire. You will pick it up and hold it to your chest. You will scream my name.

THE ENGLISH PROFESSOR
IN THE BREAKROOM

The blood in the amphitheater is mine. It leads to the break room where an additional twelve 5.56 NATO bullets have passed through my body and become lodged in the refrigerator, the microwave, the hand soap dispenser, the crucifix above the sink. It is autumn. Most of the campus is at Chapel. Through the second-story window overlooking the university parking lot and the rust-red bloom of the Appalachian Trail, you can see the student escape through the Yellow Breeches: Tall, white, a man who only became a man last summer. He carries the rifle with two hands, just like his father taught him to the first time they went deer hunting. The student prefers autumn to spring. As he enters the familiar woods, he thinks about that first buck, an easy target from the blind. He tries not to think about the story we read in class, the one about the high school student with the gun in the locker and the girl's body in the cement. He tries not to think about the look on his classmates' faces when he defended the student in the story's right to own a Moss 500. How he himself owns three and is afraid to lose them once a new president is elected. He tries not to think about his parents' attorneys, how he barely escaped expulsion, how I moved differently, slower than a wounded animal does as I escaped the amphitheater to the break room. Mostly, he thinks about that first buck. The thrill of the chase. And he is satisfied.

THE CHILD IN THE HOUSE

There was never supposed to be a body. Not in a housing development, not in a square of dirt that would become a bedroom, a place for sleep, for dreaming. I was six when he taught me his special way of playing house. He was bigger than me but too young, somehow, for his man's body. And while the weight of him has kept me breathless for decades, in my nightmares, he has no body at all, only nostrils -- strange mushrooms against overcast sky -- and footfalls in the gravel drive, too quiet to echo. Thirty years later, when I ask what I did wrong -- I had to have done something wrong, or else why it had happened so many times? -- Dr. Moran will point to the target above my head, the one given to me that afternoon in the dirt of the half-constructed bi-level. She will show me how to dismantle it. Guilt. Shame. Here, she will say, fingering my name into the damp, ready soil. This is how to live.

None of This Is Real

On shooting day 17 of 59, we find Britney behind a white shower curtain in LA General's ER, her saline-tubed arm wrapped around a black pelican case of walkie talkies. The Prius her parents cosigned for is a mangled installation of metal and smoke and craft services at the bottom of the spitless LA river. The new Air Jordans she'd been flexing at crew call on shooting day 41 of 59 are missing their treads, have been shoved into a plastic bag with her name on it hanging at the end of her hospital bed.

"She growled at us!" the tattooed nurse with the fresh undershave says. He laughs and licks at his clear retainer. "She said *they* would fire her if she didn't bring them back to work tomorrow. Who are *they*? Is it *you*? Are *you* they?" He rounds Britney's bed to the wall of machines keeping her stabilized and hydrated. He writes down a few numbers and continues the story, "I was like, girl, you got a busted collarbone, fractured hip, and subdural hematoma the size of my ass. You're *not* going to work tomorrow. You're not going to work *next month*. The only place you're going is online and to PT. That's when she lost it. She started growling and crying. Like a fucking hyena. I said *girrrrl*—" an incomprehensible page crackles over the hospital intercom—"I said *girl*, you howlin' at a deaf moon. But…the others and I…we felt bad and were like okay, whatever, we'll let her keep them in the bed if it chills her out. Once we told her that—" he brings his hand down onto the clipboard like an anvil, "*boom!—good night*. She's been down for—" he checks his notes, "*twelve* hours now?"

We thank him for his assistance and compassion for Britney. We compliment him on his nightingale forearm tattoo. When he leaves, we take the walkie talkie case and speed back towards our shooting location in Santa Monica. We make it to set ten minutes before crew call, open the walkie case. We are speechless. The radios are all charged and ready to go, which means they must have been plugged in at the hospital, which means Britney did exactly what we'd trained her to do.

*

The first time I stayed up all night to see the sunrise, I was ten.

I played *Pee Wee's Big Adventure* over and over on the 13" Magnavox in my room. My senses magnified as the night wore down, the TV taking on a fifth dimension. The whine of the VHS rewinding in the player became a song with hidden lyrics. I watched and rewatched the scene where Pee Wee and Simone huddle in the mouth of the T-Rex and wait for the new day to come. I wanted to see those impossible colors—the dawn's fiery entrance.

Just before daybreak, a fog moved in and blocked the sun. Everything looked flat, desaturated, compressed to death like an old television show. I fell asleep at my desk before lunch and dreamed I was on a train to Hollywood, part of a massive search party looking for Pee Wee's stolen bike. Everything was technicolor. Everything was beautiful and worth investigating. I woke up to the lunch bell and decided a world of color is the only kind of world worth living in. I needed to figure out how to relocate to that world, to harness its light and orchestrate its soundscapes. I needed to discover how to bring that world to the colorless one, to make them one.

I needed to learn how to make movies.

*

On shooting day 45 of 59, I let the Best Boy Electric call the martini shot and spin the dials because he is pretty to watch and after twenty hours on set, words are cotton candy silliness in my mouth.

"That's a wrap," he says, eight times, once for each department channel on the radio.

The Actors are the first to leave and take their entourage of hair and make-up artists with them in the transpo van back to base camp where they will undress and hang their wardrobe and prop bags on the back of the trailer door. They will fall asleep in the passenger seat of the sleek black Suburban escort back to the hotel and will return before the union-mandated 12-hour turnaround is up. The producers have done the math. Forced calls cost less than adding days to the shooting schedule.

I wait for the Best Boy—Juergen—at the lowered lift gate of the 18-wheel electric truck parked behind the talent trailers. He is hunched at a makeshift desk towards the front of the shipping container, purple LED lights spilling their psychedelic confetti over his black hair. He is filling out the electric department paperwork that he will give to me so I can enter it into the production report that I send to the office each night. The crew parking lot is empty except for us, a condor, and a long line of two-bangers, honeywagons and work trucks. The sun is about to rise over the Pacific Ocean.

Juergen takes his time with the pen and paper, fills each little rectangle on the matrix with a whole number and fraction to the closest twelfth. He knows I can't leave without his calculations—without him.

He means to keep me here, but he doesn't mean to keep me up. Fatigue isn't a weapon we use against each other, not on these marathon-style gigs.

We have sex in the passenger seat of his yellow X-Terra. He tells me he loves me for the first time. I tell him I have to finish the production report and give him a playful kiss on the neck.

I'm so tired I accidentally assign the camera department meal penalties to the grip department and forget to enter the mileage for our stuntman, who drove 160 miles roundtrip to set because he is terrified of flying. Two hours after Juergen called the last shot, I click send on the production report email.

I drive home full of Juergen and Red Bull and panic. It's 5:30am. The 405 is less parking lot, more drive-thru, and maybe that's why I almost miss the exit and cut too hard into the off-ramp. The retaining wall pinball-paddles me up over the embankment and back across five lanes of red and white lights. I come to a stop upside-down beneath a CBS billboard and a cement sky, suffocate into a colorless sleep.

*

In 1965, a 17-year-old boy stayed awake for 264 hours for his science fair project. On the eleventh day, he slept 14 hours and 40 minutes. The doctor supervising his high school science experiment reported no lasting physical side effects.

Within days, he could run a sub-7 5k and split half a cord of oak.

The conclusion? A body can endure. It can recover.

A person can survive without dreams.

*

After I fall asleep at the wheel, Juergen builds a living room set inside my bedroom closet. I wake up to him sitting in a director's chair beside my bed, the crackle of walkie talkie chatter everywhere.

"What's going on?" I look down at the filleted meat of my arms, the cadre of stuffed animals at the foot of my raised trundle bed, the center of which includes a fluffy orca spouting a satin banner with the words: "Life blows sometimes. Get whale soon!"

Our goateed Key Set PA, Edwin, emerges from the closet with a gift basket full of reusable hot and cold packs, trail mix, highlighters, and organic muscle balms. He parks the awkward boat of miscellany on top of my computer desk. "From the producers," he says and then disappears behind the palisade of blazers and college sweatshirts I've meticulously hung and organized by season.

I turn to Juergen, who is enthusiastically scraping the bottom out of a yogurt cup. "Orcas are dolphins."

Juergen draws the spoon across his tongue. "Huh?"

"Get 'whale'?" I say, pointing at the black and white toy. "Orcas. They're fucking dolphins."

Juergen swallows hard and sets the empty cup on the floor beside his director's chair. "Then why do they call them killer whales?"

My bedroom door opens. Our A Camera Operator and her First and Second Assistant Camera crew members pass the foot of my bed with coffee in paper to-go cups. Marcy, the Second Assistant Camera, gives me a cheeky wave before disappearing into the closet.

"Juergen, what's going on? What's happening?"

"You can work from home now," he says. "No more commute."

"What about the company moves to the Malibu house? What about the exterior shoots on days 30 to 37?"

"Rewritten. The producers didn't want to lose you," he says. Then, "your dad doesn't mind. He even helped the construction set up the flats for a few of the club scene interiors. Your closet is much bigger than you think it is."

I'm twenty-seven, but I've been living with my parents in Venice Beach to save money for a down-payment on a bungalow in North Hollywood. I'm not sure how Juergen got here or managed to fit eighty-five crew members and their gear between the secret library of R.L Stine books and a Ponderosa my dad and I built when I was eight, but I'm actually more concerned about Juergen seeing the shameful artifacts of my later childhood—badminton trophies, unfinished crucifix lanyards, a paper shrine devoted to Leonardo DiCaprio and Baz Luhrmann's *Romeo & Juliet*.

He knows too much now.

I can't afford to lose this assistant directing gig. I need the union days. I can't afford to lose my health insurance. Especially since the arrhythmias started. Who can afford to pay out-of-pocket for an EKG every month? On no income?

A small part of me holds out hope that if I can make it through the next few weeks of this shoot, I might have enough reserve to take a month off and finish my feature script. I might have time to make it good, to get it agented, to land something that could get me out of these brutal, endless, grinding days of platforming someone else's dream.

"Oh my god," I say. I grab the clipboard Juergen has placed by my pillow and scan the call sheet I don't remember completing but must have because—there it is—my signature at the bottom. "My parents are going to kill me."

"I told you," Juergen says, "Your dad's cool with it." Then, "It was tricky to figure out crew parking and where to put the work trucks. Your neighbor with the surfing Jesus sculpture screamed at Lily in Wardrobe because her Jeep was blocking the view of oncoming traffic and she almost got T-boned by the Sound van rolling up. But it's all good now. Locations and Production secured a basecamp three blocks away, in the old Blockbuster parking lot."

*

Shooting day 48 of 59. Juergen says the producers don't want me to have a walkie talkie. Really, it's doctor's orders. They say a surveillance in my ear will make the head trauma worse, which will slow recovery. Even though he isn't in my department, Juergen has been assigned to communicate between me and the crew. He creates a small working desk out of my pink six-drawer vanity in the corner of the room by clamping some black lights to the mirror and using my exercise ball as a chair.

"I can't work like this," I say.

"You don't need to work. It is all being done for you," Juergen says, bouncing and smiling at me in the mirror.

I'm in bed, but I don't sleep.

*

Shooting day 51 of 59. I see things. Shadow puppets in my peripheral vision. Crew members I don't know. I tell Edwin to bring me a sticky note with the day players' names on it, and he disappears into the closet for hours at a time, only to return with C-47s (clothespins) clipped together in varying configurations of a voodoo dolls and effigies.

My hands flicker like a television screen. Here they are. There they go.

Nine hours into our day, and two hours since I dismissed Edwin and his evil art creations, Juergen comes in from the hallway carrying a sandwich on one of my parents' stoneware plates.

"Your mom sends her best—and your favorite sandwich," Juergen approaches the bed and holds out the plate.

"So now you know," I say.

"Liverwurst and pickles. She asked if I wanted one," he says, "but I told her I only eat animals from the chest up."

"So by that logic you'll eat brains but you won't eat thighs?"

Juergen leans in close and whispers, "Do you know what a liver does?"

I swipe the plate from Juergen and set it by the glass and brass touch lamp on my side table. The room ripples like a pond in a breeze, a little bit of color escaping into the closet with each successive ebb.

"You okay?" Juergen asks.

"Where's Britney?"

"Britney who?"

"The set PA who crashed her—" I stop. Smoke is wafting in from the closet door.

Juergen catches my gaze, "They're prepping the dream sequence where Meredith kills Dolores so that she can have Herman all to herself. Jimmy's going a little wild on the fog machine, so I'm thinking of tripping a fuse on him."

"What am I even doing, Juergen? What is going on?"

"You're working. Recovering and working."

"I'm sitting in a twin bed. The twin bed where I lost my virginity to Brian Thum and fingered Kelsey Milhouse."

Juergen grins. "Liverwurst aside, the more I learn about you—"

"There's an eighty-person film crew making an entire season of episodic television inside of my closet, and I'm just sitting here with a clipboard I can't read and disappearing hands." I look at him, "Why am I here? *Am* I here? Am I asleep? Is this some kind of experiment to see how much *they* can fuck with me before I totally lose it and fold?"

Juergen looks at me with genuine confusion. "Just what you said. We're making a show. You crashed your car, and Randy decided to bring the show to you. To be safe. To get it done, too. But mostly to be safe. I don't know. Maybe they also want to avoid a lawsuit. Actually, now that I think about it—"

"This isn't real. None of this is real."

"Remember when we did the telenovela gig down in San Diego?" Juergen asks. "We used our housing stipends to buy all that speed and ended up in Vegas with only our phones and wallets? We laid on the floor of the Bellagio, under those huge glass flower sculptures they had on the ceiling, people walking around us in their Louis Vuittons, holding martinis and shit, until security came?" He laughs. "You kept telling them 'none of this is real.' You kept repeating it, over and over, all the way back up to our room where we sat in the shower for like two hours. Those security fuckers were laughing at you, but I knew you were talking about something else…"

"I repeat myself when I'm smashed," I say.

"Maybe," he says. "Or maybe the truth caught you with your guard down and was trying to make itself heard."

He unties his size fourteen Wolverine work boot and pulls out a small bottle of Becherovka, which I haven't seen since I broke my foot behind a frozen church in Hradčanská, Prague. He puts the green glass to his lips and smiles.

"I'm losing it," I say. "None of this makes sense," and then, "Where did you get that?"

Juergen inspects the bottle, as if seeing it for the first time. "You know…I don't know. Props department? To be honest, weird stuff like this has been happening to me a lot a lot now."

"Doesn't that bother you?"

He shrugs and takes a careful sip, "Not really."

Becherovka is a secret bitter. Vintage enough to seem exotic, but not ancient. As he continues to sip, the centuries-old breeze of cinnamon and clove stirs memory from my body and projects it on the back of my bedroom door: Me, standing on the Charles Bridge, peering into the scintillating brilliance of the Vltava. I don't have a camera or a phone or a motive. I don't need to capture the moment's simple beauty by suffocating it into artistic preservation. I am simply present. Ambitionless. Relishing the bitters burning through my empty stomach, the fiery colors of the world I thought had abandoned me that night when I was ten.

Juergen sees the projection, too. He climbs into bed next to me, and we watch the POV shot play out. He doesn't know it is my vision, but it doesn't matter. That's the subjective magic of film. The suspension of disbelief. The reason we are here.

He holds the bottle under my nose and rolls the wet

glass across my lips. He strokes my hair while I sip myself into the past. The bedroom corners soften into merengue. Panic, the ever-ticking clock in my chest, lifts into the atmosphere. The gentle, flickering water montage on my door continues its interminable dance.

Juergen rises like a kite, tapes a blue gel over my bedroom window. Venice Beach becomes the Challenger Deep.

"The sun can pretend it's the moon now," Juergen says, sailing back to me, sweeping over the narrow shore of my body.

Everything is water now. We kiss the soft sand of each other's stomachs. We drown beneath blue sheets.

Hammers and power tools and periodic laughter indicate that the crew inside the closet is erecting a fourth wall.

Juergen slips his thumb into my mouth and drags his teeth across my chest. We listen for open radios, try to gauge how much time we have before they're ready to shoot the scene.

"You'll miss the safety meeting," I mumble into his neck.

I can't stop saying the things I am being paid of say. Thousands of hours on set will do that. It's not the art that replaces the person, it's the monotony. But there is still this humanness pulsing between my legs, feelings being felt without words to flatten them into comprehension. A library of feelings waiting for desperate researching. And Juergen does that. He crawls up inside of me with an eager mind. He opens the secret door to my inner home and peruses the bookshelves of my soul. He trips and falls through the threshold separating my living room and kitchen and pores over the secrets I keep hidden in the expired condiments in my refrigerator door. He lies naked in my bed, masturbates to the sound of me laughing, and then runs a bath until it overflows and I'm flooded from the inside out.

When he leaves, the emptiness feels different. Lived in.

When he leaves, I open my eyes and see that I am alone and the bedroom door is just a door. The memory has passed. Everything is quiet.

I can't remember the last time I had company over.

I can't remember the day I stopped living inside of my body.

*

A 37-year-old Boom Operator in Phoenix, Arizona, collapses in the middle of a take on the seventh day of shooting the remake of the fifth installment in the *Saw* series. The Unit Production Manager, trying to make a comeback after two failed Tom Arnold pilots, tells two Dolly Grips to carry the woman out to the empty field behind the sound stage so that the Set Medic can do compressions until paramedics arrive. The UPM hands the boom pole to the Production Assistant who was, unbeknownst to her, just out behind the generators doing whip-its with Craft Services and the Props Master.

As the actors reset to their starting positions, the UPM leans over to the Locations Manager. "Is there a way for us to contact the ambulance and ask them not to use their sirens?" she whispers. "Actually, if you don't mind standing down the street so you can flag them down, we catch the trucks before they get here, and that way they won't ruin the takes we need to get in before lunch."

*

Juergen puts his mouth over mine. Everything tastes like cinnamoned pine and blood. A voice crackles through the soft plastic surveillance piece dangling from his ear: "Five minutes until picture."

"You know that means ten minutes," he whispers. "Kevin will forget to jam the slate. Bonita's going to ask Roberto to give her a line read again. We have time."

There's only so much time for us to do what we need to do. The black gaff tape he uses to fix me to the headboard is paper thin, so I am very careful not to struggle or reach for him. We both know my bondage is one part illusion, two parts compliance, but I don't know if Juergen can feel my growing unease.

"Do you remember Charles Shaughnessy?" I ask. Juergen wraps my left wrist to the bed frame one more time and throws a glance at the closet to see if anyone from the crew is spying on us through the open sliding doors. "He was the dad on *The Nanny*. The British guy?"

"Yeah, I gaffed a life insurance commercial with him in Rancho Cucamonga."

"He saved me from electrocution once."

"Only once?" Juergen runs his lips from my wrists down to my chest.

"We were filming a pilot about a yacht club."

Juergen looks up, holds my face in his sturdy hands, "This is exactly why you can never go back to low-budget shows. If I'd been there, it wouldn't have been an issue."

"No, no. It wasn't an electrical department issue," I tell him. "If anything, it was a locations issue. We nearly capsized when a pod of blue whales breached nearby. I fell overboard into a school of electric stargazers. Charles jumped into the tender boat and came back to get me. He was a hero, but the script was terrible."

Juergen kisses my forehead and looks into my eyes, "This is what we do. It's crazy, but it's life. We live for this shit."

*

Before the famous actor shot and killed the up-and-coming cinematographer on a low-budget western outside of Santa Fe, New Mexico, the camera department protested the producers' decision to deny them housing, forcing them to gamble with their exhaustion and commute hours to and from set on a desolate stretch of road. The Producers, modern-day Narcissuses powered on lithium batteries and viral Tik Toks, ordered black long-sleeve shirts with the phrase "You can sleep when you're dead" silkscreened across the front.

The morning of the murder, as the Camera Crew were collecting their lenses and monitors and preparing to disembark the runaway train of a production—for their dignity and humanity and livelihoods!—the Executive Producer paces the equipment staging area, bundle of burning sage raised high, and chants a mantra he purchased from @nativemedwogoddess, a supposed Dakota Nations medicine woman on Venmo, the night before. When he finishes the smudging ritual, he circles the dispersing Camera Crew, mumbling and scrolling his phone, "You feel that? You feel those low vibrations just *evaporating* right out of here?"

*

Day 53 of 59. My vision is crowded with floaters. Translucent cobwebs and tiny shadow puppets all using my corneas as a dance floor. I can't read the small text on the call sheet anymore, so Juergen sings it to me, line by line.

"Production notes: No open-toed shoes. Forced calls no longer prohibited. Meal penalties as needed. Must start-work-finish all principals today. No open radios on set. Safety meeting to be held thirty minutes after call. Must wrap out of location by 5am. Submit your NCAA brackets to Sammy by noon. Don't drink and drive."

The bedroom ceiling light flickers and goes dark. The plastic stars my parents bought me during our trip to Lick Observatory when I was eight form a harrowing constellation across the flat white sky. Two words:

BE FAMOUS.

*

The Segment Producer from *The Daily Show* is someone I know from film school in LA. I slept with her boyfriend before he was her boyfriend, took his virginity before I knew he was a virgin. I liked her a lot when we were in the same Punch-Up Techniques for TV Comedy Writing class. She had the dirtiest jokes and the stealthiest callbacks. She is Canadian and married to a cybersecurity expert who works from home and takes care of their 4-month-old daughter. I know this from browsing her Instagram posts, which she strategically adds to maybe once every three months.

I run into the Segment Producer from *The Daily Show* on a weekend trip to New York City to watch a one-man stand-up show I've been asked to help produce as a web series for a new streaming service. I've just left the staged reading and am headed towards my Air bnb in Chelsea, rewinding the tape in my head, feeling anxiously com-

THEY MORE THAN BURNED

mitted even though the topical jokes about abortion and gun violence and #metoo drew more ire than laughs, when I hear a woman call my name from across the intersection. It's a pleasant chance encounter. Organic and far enough removed from the film school days that I can set aside any shame or guilt I might still have over the regret I felt every time I saw her with the man whose virginity I took and didn't realize I'd been in love with, until it was too late.

"Congratulations on becoming a mom," I tell her.

"Oh my god, *shhhh!*" she says, ducking between me and a cement apartment staircase. "You're going to get me fired!"

"What are you talking about?" I look behind us, genuinely convinced that she had seen someone materialize out of the ether at the mention of motherhood.

My friend rises slowly, smooths her beige suit jacket down over an impossibly flat postpartum stomach. "Ever since our post-production supervisor was fired for having twins, we've decided not to talk about Skylar until she is in kindergarten."

"We?"

"Me and my husband."

"Kindergarten. That's like five years, Debbie."

"It goes so much faster than you think," she says with more joy than despair. "How about you? Do you have any...?"

"I don't even have a person, Debbie," I say.

The Daily Show Segment Producer's face relaxes into sudden disconnect. She checks her phone and starts drifting up 8th Avenue. "I have a meeting with the censors in twenty minutes and need to go. It was so great running into you. Let's get together the next time you're in the city!"

"Hey, Debbie," I call. "Why did they fire her? Did she

miss days at work? Stop showing up?"

"She was falling asleep in the sound mixes. And at the spotting sessions. And at the studio screenings. They said it was sleep deprivation and blamed the babies." She gives me a knowing look. "You know who they really blamed."

*

Shooting Day 59 of 59. I've forgotten the color of sky, the elevation of dreams.

"Striking!" The closet casts a rectangle of cold gray light across the bed. The sheets are soaking wet and smell like asphalt and gasoline.

The traffic noise escalates into a rainless thunder.

Juergen and I are separated by three lanes of traffic. He is a small figurine standing by the miniature closet door in my now infinite room. He cinches his work belt and waves at me. Even at this distance, his body is the exact shape of my longing.

I start to cry.

"What's wrong?" he shouts. Two U-Hauls and a funeral procession pass between us.

"I don't think I'm sleeping," I say.

"It's all sleeping and being awake. It's always been like that."

"No, this is different," I say.

The bedroom door opens, and two paramedics walk in and set two duffle bags on the floor by the open closet. They wait for a break in the traffic and jog over to me, immediately begin to tear me free from the headboard.

The Female Paramedic takes me under the arms, the Male Paramedic grabs me by the shins, and on the count of three, they hoist me off the bed and lie me on the glass-and-aluminum-littered asphalt of the freeway median. The

Female Paramedic sprints to the exit shoulder and hands the defibrillator power cord to Juergen, who plugs it into a black electrical box at the foot of the dresser right next to the closet door.

Juergen, looking into the closet, into the cool gray light, speaks confidently into the surveillance microphone, "Tell Rick we can power fucking Beijing if he needs us to. We'll get him a second sun, simulate a forest fire, whatever the fuck he wants."

"You dozed off," the Male Paramedic says. His eyes are shiny nickels that flash blue as someone turns the key light towards him. Desi from Hair and Makeup flies in, dabs a little paintbrush across my lips and blows a tear stick into my eyes to moisten them up.

"Looks are good," she says into the surveillance microphone clipped to her romper. She winks at me and jogs away, smacking her gum and zipping her fanny pack as she goes.

"What's happening?" I manage.

Someone dips a boom mic over my head. "Can we get a sound check real quick?"

"What?"

The Male Paramedic lifts his mouth to the shotgun microphone and sings the horn solo from "Tequila" by The Champs.

The Boom Operator, a day player I don't recognize, gives a thumbs up and the Male Paramedic turns back to me, smiling, "We're about to get going. Just waiting on the defibrillator to charge."

A colorless sun crests over the CBS billboard, casts its gray beams across my totaled car, the morning traffic.

I'm not struggling to breathe, but the Male Paramedic places an oxygen mask over my face anyway. I can hear the

First Assistant Camera person call the shot to my left, but I can't see her—"Episode 59, Scene 7, Take One. A and B, common mark—soft sticks." A gentle clap indicates she's clapped the slate.

There's a brief pause. Someone calls out, "Set!" The Director says, "Action!"

I start to cry, "Am I dead?"

The Male Paramedic strokes my hair with genuine concern, his previously blue eyes now haunting daguerreotypes of silver and milk. "Don't worry, sweetheart. You just hang in there, okay? We're gonna get you back up and running in no time. I promise."

"But I'm not…"

The Female Paramedic enters screen left with the charged defibrillator, hits her mark so that she's a shadow perfectly backlit by the rising sun. "Charged to 900," she says.

"900 volts?" I panic as they continue to talk around me.

"Good God, we're losing her," the Male Paramedic cries, quickly taking up the paddles.

"Are we clear, Jack?" the Female Paramedic asks.

The Male Paramedic pauses, feigns intense reflection as he remembers his line. He looks deeply into my eyes until he finds it. "Damn it," he says finally, standing up, pulling a white shower curtain closed between us. "We've lost her."

When the Alcoholic Falls from the Sky

When the alcoholic falls from the sky, there is no equation for calculating where she will land because, in every story but this one, she never does.

*

When the time comes to surrender, it won't feel like rock bottom because, in the end, it's not about the rock or the bottom—death has no altitude.

Instead, it will feel like another long drive home. It will feel like a balloon that can hold more air, like if you could just turn yourself inside out, there you will finally be.

*

I am two months sober when the first snow falls. I meet strangers in night churches and witness testimonies about lifted obsession. I eat the candy and cry into the coffee. I don't tell anyone that I am afraid obsession is all I have.

Stay in the middle of the herd, Steve M. says one night, pulling a wallet from his back pocket. He's wearing an Akubra cattleman hat and aviators and doesn't crowd me the way other men in these rooms have. From a bundle of cards secured with a rubber band, he offers me a hand-drawn picture of buffalo near a mesa, some are grazing, some are frolicking—do buffalo frolic?—and some are, by all obvious artistic intentions, *lost*. As I shovel a pouch of M&Ms into my mouth, Steve hands me a figurine and points to the bottom of the drawing where a solitary brown splotch wanders near an uncertain scribble labeled "cliff."
You find yourself here, you call someone who can help get you back to the herd. If no one answers, you put that under your tongue so you

can't talk yourself into anything stupid.

*

I fell 18,000 feet and still needed more. Codeine, cocaine, Klonopin. Cooking sherry, Listerine and Coricidin. Only another alcoholic can understand: If I'd known the last drink would be my last, I never would've stopped.

*

When a helicopter falls from the sky in the night three streets away from our Cape Cod, no one is there to see it except God. Nothing is there to stop it except the jungle gym and a sugar maple, some half-bloomed matchsticks of golden rod. I'm in a bed that isn't mine, dreaming I am on the wrong flight to Alaska, the empty fuselage hydrolicking over Saskatchewan. I'm drunk and stanning the flight attendant and his tiny bottles of Crown Royal. Like all drunk dreams, I'm using with the intent to fuck someone. I tell the attendant that if we are going to die, I need him to come inside of me first. Dream drinking is not unlike real drinking. In both, obsession and excess unite, blaze, flashover. The cabin lights flicker. The flight attendant abandons his cart and takes me across a row of empty seats. He tells me the turbulence scares him, so I pull him all the way inside of me like a secret, explain that we will be transcending the darkness soon, that we are flying so fast, we are silencing the sound before it can catch us.

The orgasm wakes me up, and the bedsheets are soaked like they used to be. I get up before the kids and run seven miles through the fog, unsure if I'm still sober. At mile two, I find the propeller in a ditch where I used to dump my bottles in neatly tied grocery bags. At mile three, I find the smaller-than-expected exoskeleton emptied of its passengers. At mile five, I'm convinced that I'm drunk and the attendant is still inside of me and that shame is prophecy.

*

Google "things falling from the sky" and you can frighten your obsession into distraction. Boiled bats, venison, spiders, suitcases, starfish, baby shoes, blood oranges, needles, and tree frogs—

I am not so much afraid to fly as I am to fall. Physics promises us that everything, even clouds, come back to earth. All bodies have a terminal velocity. Nothing escapes physics. Except God. And black holes. And maybe a little bit of the Devil.

*

When a 2014 Jetta falls from the sky, downing two telephone poles and leveling several cement mailboxes, I am asleep in a bed that isn't mine, dreamless. I am expecting lightning when I descend the stairs and emerge barefoot into the asphalt darkness. At first, the capsized vehicle in a constellation of picket fencing and windshield glass looks like every car I've ever owned, but as I move closer, I can see I'm not the one at fault. One neighbor is picking up pieces of mailbox from four houses down. I approach a heavyset man in a monikered shirt bending over the driver's side window. With the streetlights out, it is so dark, I can't see who is inside.

"Are they okay?" I whisper, thinking he is real, thinking I am not dreaming.

The man looks at me, confused, as if I'm a cloud to be passed through, and though I have never seen him before, I know who he is, that there is no one inside the car, that he is still falling.

The electricity is out when I get home. Everyone is still asleep. I salivate and think maybe I am too. I don't know.

By the light of my phone, I dig through the shit in my Steelcase—candy wrappers, mini DV tapes, safety pins, shot glasses, phone chargers, photos, and air fresheners—until I find the tiny buffalo. I place it under my tongue. It tastes like royal pine and sheet metal, the latex hard but clinical. I say "fall" and it comes out "fool." I say "shit" and it comes out "sit." Because I know what happens when I don't follow directions, I drop to the floor. I wrangle the tiny buffalo with my tongue—count and recount its stubborn legs as I turn my body into a human airstrip. I wait for the ceiling to crack open, for grace to make its emergency landing.

Work Release

They don't teach you this in college. Or Hollywood. Watch. This is how you do it. First, take the full-sized towel. Keep it folded in half. Be sure to check for stains, hairs, holes, tears. Pick off what you can. You can use your fingers, but I carry scissors just in case.

Now, fold the sides in a quarter of the way. Just like that. Yeah. Then roll it—top to bottom, until the sides come together tight, like a pair of lips. Exactly—just like that, but tighter—like they're keeping a secret.

Next, fold those over. See that? Now you've got four legs and can start on the head. For that, you use a hand towel—not a washcloth. The washcloth is too small. It's best to get one of the older towels. The new ones are too soft and don't keep shape as well.

Okay. So keep this one folded in half, too. Put your finger in the middle at the top, and roll each side tight. Looks kinda like a fucked up paper airplane now, right? Okay, turn it over. Roll the flat end down and then bend back and tuck. Place it on top of the body you made. You can stretch the trunk out however you want. Toni always has the trunk down, but I think that looks sad. Looks like he's lonely, like Dumbo after they put his mom in jail.

With mine, I like to have the trunk up in the air like he's reaching for a snack or saying hi. You know—I make them at home, too. Layla loves them. I make a whole parade for her. That's what a group of them is called, did you know that? Sounds so happy, right? That means they should *look* happy, too. That's why I put its trunk up in the air and not between the legs like Toni does. She makes better swans though. She's got this way of making their necks look perfect.

Here, you want some? That's right—I forgot. You don't drink. I tried that once. Life was boring. It sounds fucked up when I say that shit out loud. But it's true. There's nothing else to do around here. Winters are brutal.

Okay, now you try.

Pause.

Don't tell Toni what I said about her making better swans. That shit will go straight to her head. Hey, that's looking good. You're doing real good.

Pause.

I've never seen an elephant before. Have you? Is it weird to have a favorite animal you've never seen in real life?

Don't worry about that. The ears are the hardest part. Too much sticking out and the head falls off. Try again. Use your finger to get a tighter roll on the trunk.

I found this elephant sanctuary in Tennessee. All elephants, nothing else. Layla loves elephants. Could give a shit about tigers or rhinos, so it's the perfect place for us to go. I've never told her I haven't seen one, but how cool would that be? For us to see an elephant for the first time? Together?

Pause.

Holy shit, that looks great. Must mean I'm a good teacher, right? God, it feels so good to sit. What else do we need to do? Did you check the drawers? Make sure they're empty. People leave all kinds of weird shit in there—cock rings, needles, Air Pods—I forget to check all the time. No, no. The Bible stays. People need something to read when they're bored.

Pause.

You sure you don't want some? It'll make the day go

faster. Alright, we should probably replace the toilet paper roll. You remember how to fold the ends? Yeah, triangles and a little accordion fan. You do it. I'll watch.

Pause.

Perfect. You're a pro. What do you think? Do we need to sweep the floors, or do they look good to you? I don't always sweep, but I disinfect the shit out of the bathroom. I've got this thing about showers.

Pause.

Okay, you mop and I'll sit a minute. I never sit, but it's so fucking hot. You know we used to be able to swim in the pool. But then Chris brought his whole family up and they got cranked and drunk and started a fire in the brush near Stillhouse. Freaked out some Jehovah's witnesses who were on their way to a convention in Philly.

Pause.

That looks great. Damn. You're a pro now. Hey, turn on that AC and let's sit a minute. I never sit, but we can't start stayovers until ten, so we might as well take a break, and it's hot as fuck.

Pause.

So I found a nice hotel pretty close to the elephant sanctuary. Like, me and Layla could walk there if we wanted to. Not too expensive and had pretty good reviews. I'm so picky now that I work here. I get anxious when I walk into a room for the first time. I always expect to see where someone didn't do their job. I'm always looking for hairs and stains. I know you're only here until you get your license back, but prepare for all future hotel stays to be ruined.

Pause.

This place, though—the one next to the sanctuary— looks *real* nice. Way nicer than here. I bet they even have fitted sheets. None of this hospital-style fold bullshit. I keep telling Kelly that we'd be able to flip twice as many rooms if we had fitted sheets, but no one listens to me.

When I get that vacation time—and some extra cash—Layla and me will sleep on beds someone else made. We'll wake up and eat pancakes and sausage and waffles with ice cream on top, and then we'll get dressed in a set of those dorky mother-daughter matching getups and we'll go see the elephants having their parade.

Pause.

You sure you don't want any? I won't tell anyone.

Pause.

Damn. That's a good elephant. Even better than mine.

Not Everyone in that Facebook Photo You Posted of Yellow House Is Dead

Sixteen years after the towers burn, Joe calls to say he's still alive and that not everyone in that Facebook photo I posted of Yellow House is dead. Anita, Shoshona, Shawnta, and Johnboy—they're alive, too.

Although, he says. *Some of us more alive than others.*

It's a wintry 6pm outside, but feels later, darker. My husband is teaching a dual-enrolled night class on Judaism at the college, and my kids are huddled around their tablet screen in the living room. I'm not prepared to talk to a ghost, even if he has been haunting my waking and dream lives for more than a decade now.

We should go back to visit. Invite everyone.

I tell Joe they leveled what was left of Yellow House into a U-Store parking lot ten years ago. I've already gone back and counted the painted graves.

"I'm still having nightmares about the fire," I say. "I keep imagining the line of oil trucks passing my house on their way to the refinery exploding like cherry bombs."

Imagine having those kinds of nightmares all day, every day, he says. His voice is still as smooth and controlled as it was before he deployed all those years ago. *There's a reason why all those jarheads we knew from Pendleton started killing themselves.*

I want to tell Joe about the other nightmares that weren't nightmares, like the morning I drove drunk to the middle of a strawberry field and prayed over a revolver while my children napped on the couch in front of our TV.

"It's been fifty-six days since I've had a drink," I say. "But today, I thought about one. I'm thinking about one right now."

I heard you made a short documentary about us.

"I did."

That you're trying to sell a longer one.

"Not trying. They came to me. They saw the film at Tribeca and came at me with a deal memo. I guess they think our stories will sell."

Then sell them. Sell the shit out of them. Someone needs to profit off of this bullshit.

"It feels like I'm selling myself, to be honest. I don't know. I don't trust them. I'm in a weird place right now. They're flying me back to LA next week to screen some of the rough cut. It's…rough."

I heard you're writing another book, too.

"Trying," I say. "The Tribeca documentary was just a snapshot. I have so much tape from those days and used so little for that short. But there are things that just don't translate to screen, you know? Things they don't want to show." Then, "I know how this goes."

I heard about what happened to you in Hollywood.

"Everyone heard."

Is that why you ran away with a high school teacher and moved to butt-fuck nowhere?

"I fell in love."

Lucky bastard.

"I remember seeing you and Danny."

Yeah, we all know how that ended.

"You mean how you <u>asked him</u> to end it?"

I know you've seen the tape. But that's not how it went down.

"How did it go down?"

I'm not at liberty to say. Then, *Do you know what they do to guys like me in the Army?*

"Joe, why did you even enlist?"

I was bored. I wanted to stop thinking about killing myself.

My kids have finished their dinner and slipped upstairs to their YouTube videos and Legos.

"I keep writing stories about you," I say. "I don't know why." Then, "Every time I sit down, you're right there on the page. I don't know if it's you or the idea of you. JP's there, too. And Danny—"

Maybe you're in love with me. Are you in love with me?

"—I can't see what it is."

What what is?

"What I'm making."

I thought you were making a film.

"I was making a film," I say. "But it's not just a film anymore. It's become something bigger. Messier. An archive of notes and people. Of grief. And fire. So much fire. *Everything* is on fire."

That would be a good title. Everything is on fire.

"Joe."

I tried to fuck you once.

"I know. I remember."

I thought about fucking you a lot.

"Joe…"

Joe takes a long drag of something. The lit end of whatever he is smoking crackles softly in my ear, reminding me of a time before time.

I tried everything I could not to love that bastard.

"Like joining the Army."

That may have been my greatest way of trying, but all it did was fuck me up more. We had some good years after I came back from deployment—

"Before the fire?"

Joe takes another long drag and exhales, laughing. It begins to snow. I watch my reflection become trapped in the storm.

Hey—

"Joe, why did you tell Danny to start the fire?"

—*I want you to do something for me.*

"You disappeared. You can't just disappear, not into thin air."

It gets lonely—

"You had to have gone somewhere. Where did you go?"

What do you mean where did I go? I didn't go anywhere. I'm right here. Hey—

"Were you the one who told tell Danny to film it? Or was that his idea?"

Hey, he says again.

"What?"

Send me a nude.

"No."

Why not? It gets so lonely here.

"Where is here?" I ask.

M—

The line goes dead.

I let myself feel the stillness for a moment before slipping into my husband's boots. I slide the chain from the door and step out into snow falling like ash across our driveway.

My phone vibrates. It's a photo with no text, a pixelated webcam headshot with the focus set to the basement's wood-paneled walls in the background. The long white smudge in the foreground is a face too close to the camera. Despite the low-fi motion blur, I know it's Joe and am filled with longing, not for Joe—not the love of Danny's life, the soft anarchist. It's a bigger, more abstract longing than that.

For time. Memory. Touch. Suspension of disbelief

and consciousness. One more eternal summer. One more moment of before.

An oil truck rumbles past, rattling the bones of our half-broken wind chimes. I stare at the blank square of my phone and wonder what else I can say to a dead man who thinks he's still alive.

Rough Cut Screening with the Network Executive Who Thinks He's About to LAUNCH YOUR CAREER

INT. WARNER MEDIA - OFFLINE EDITING BAY - DAY

A little darker than usual. Amber is again in the pilot seat, navigating various editing menus to get the playback settings just right.

Peter, much more informal, loose in posture, has abandoned his all-black turtleneck wardrobe for jeans and a Bob Dylan's Theme Time Radio Hour T-shirt. His signature five-day stubble is gone.

> PETER
> I got a DUI once. Ten years ago. It wasn't a huge deal. I did community service and traffic school. I paid the fine. Does that mean I have a problem?

> AMBER
> Peter, I can't answer that.

> PETER
> We don't know each other well enough.
> AMBER
> Did you watch the rough cut Abby and I did of the Yellow House footage with—

PETER
I'd like to get to know you
better.

Amber plays the script back in her head.
She doesn't want to encourage Peter. She
doesn't want to engage him either.

AMBER
(placating)
A lot can happen in ten years.

Peter sits a little taller in his chair.

PETER
A lot <u>has</u> happened. I mean,
we're going to kill it at the
Emmy's this year.

AMBER
I saw the announcement in
Variety this morning.
Congratulations.

PETER
Thank you. Thank you. That
makes fifteen noms since I
joined the network five <u>years</u>
ago. Not a record. I'm no ██████
██████. That fucking prick--

AMBER
Well, you're obviously doing
<u>something</u> right.

PETER
To be honest, I feel like I
spend most of my time placing

irons in the fire. Moments like this — with you...watching the vision evolve and come together. It's a good reminder of why I do this.

> AMBER
> I hope I can deliver.

Peter grabs the arm of Amber's chair. Turns her so that she is facing him and pulls himself into her space. It's like watching someone trying to fit the wrong shape into an opening in Tetris. Peter goes through a series of starts and restarts, trying to find how to dramatize this moment.

He leans in close enough to kiss her. With the editing console against the back of her chair, Amber has nowhere to go. She holds her breath.

> PETER
> (quietly)
> Amber. I --
> (then)
> Look. Roth has faith in you... which means I have faith in you. You are more than enough. You are brilliant. So there's no reason you shouldn't have faith in yourself.

Peter leans back, allowing Amber to turn back to the playback monitor.

ON THE MONITOR

A BLACK AND WHITE freeze frame CLOSEUP of
16-YEAR-OLD AMBER, sitting on the floor,
leaning against the side of a couch. This
is YELLOW HOUSE.

> AMBER
> --it's really hard.

> PETER
> Why?

> AMBER
> I've been here before.

> PETER
> I know. But look, this time is
> different.

> AMBER
> Is it?

> PETER
> Look at me, Amber. Look me in
> the eyes. The eyes don't lie.

Amber swivels, flashes Peter a look that
says she's been more than accommodating,
that she's tired of accommodating. The
emotional tension is 100% on his side of
the rope, and she's about to let go. She's
at the breaking point. Again. And she
doesn't want a repeat of history. All
those years she lost because of--

Peter proceeds, oblivious.

                    PETER (CONT'D)
I'm   telling   you   it's
different. You need to trust
me. Can you trust me?

                    AMBER
Honestly? I don't know.

                    PETER
You "don't know"?

                    AMBER
I've   spent   so   long   being
afraid.

Peter knows what Amber means. He's not as
oblivious as he looked a moment ago. But
Peter doesn't like how the conversation
has   shifted.   He   was   confident   he'd
performed his empathy flawlessly. Amber
turns back to the editing timeline, checks
some meta data on an unused clip in the
media bin.

                    PETER
Hey, you like my shirt?

                    AMBER
        (without looking)
Sure.

                    PETER
I know him, you know.

                    AMBER
Really. Is that so.

                    PETER
          Yeah. You like him?

Amber gives Peter's shirt a quick look and
turns back to the monitor.

                    AMBER
          Who doesn't like Dylan?

                    PETER
          You'd be surprised how many
          people hate his guts.

Amber tilts the playback monitor towards
Peter.

                    AMBER
          I've got everything cued up if
          you're ready.

                    PETER
          Dylan made legends. Practic-
          ally invented rock-stars. He
          is like a fucking god. Like
          creator of the music universe
          kind of god.
               (then)
          You just say the magic word,
          Amber, and I'll get you
          tickets.
               (and)
          Maybe we could go to one of his
          shows together.

Amber continues to talk over her shoulder.

                    AMBER
          What about Kiki?

PETER
Kiki?

BOOM! - obliviousness obliterated.
Peter's eyes recalibrate. He takes Amber
in. Runs his hand awkwardly over the
grizzle that is no longer there.

PETER (CONT'D)
Yeah...yeah--she's not into
live music. No, she'd rather be
boiled alive in a hot yoga room
than see Dylan in concert.

Peter pulls a small suede coin purse from
the pocket of a black blazer hanging over
the back of his chair. He offers it to
Amber, who takes it, frowning.

AMBER
What's this?

PETER
Open it.

Amber shoots Peter a distrustful look,
tries to hand it back.

AMBER
That's okay. I think I'll pass.

PETER
You won't regret it.

Peter leans back, folds his hands on top
of his head. His body relaxes. His legs
swing open. Amber, distrustful but
ultimately curious, unzips the purse.

She peers achingly into the soft black
leather --

-- and then GASPS.

                              CUT TO BLACK.

They ask for the truth, and when it comes, they're prepared to eradicate it. Sharpie in one hand, duct tape in the other—tasers and roofies in the cup holders of their electric cars. When it comes to truth-telling, they've got a dozen lawyers on retainer. Cash payoffs ready in the pipeline.

*

I never saw ████████████ fucking boys behind the trailers like the ████ documentary said. To be honest, I didn't see much of ██ when he wasn't on set. When I was running color pages from the writers' room down to the department heads, he was either chain smoking near the elephant door or choreographing punchlines with ████ ████ in rehearsals.

That doesn't mean the stories aren't true.

Some stories are more believable before you've seen the footage. It sounds counterintuitive, but sometimes bringing a story to life can make it disappear.

I know what it's like to disappear.

I know the exact places where erasure hurts most.

*

You smile at me over the top of your lidless paper coffee cup. The steam's curly marginalia annotates your lips.

"Do you ever wonder what could have been *if you had just…let it happen?*"

*

I was long gone by the time ████ grew out of his baby cheeks and got baptized by that YouTube pastor. I got drunk and crashed my 4-Runner the season Hollywood flatlined and stopped filming and Sheen went to rehab.

I wanted to go back to assistant directing. I stepped foot on a soundstage and pivoted. I was too suicidal to work. By the time ███████ negotiated $700,000 per episode for ██████ to join season nine, I was 2,900 miles away, attempting to redraw the parts of myself that had been erased. I had a daughter and a haunted closet full of ██████'s paper jokes, likely worth millions of dollars per page. When I couldn't recreate what I'd lost, I started anaesthetizing my amputations with bottles I kept in the center console, behind paint cans in the unfinished mudroom. I didn't know yet that some laughter doesn't require shedding blood, that phantom limbs can ache like a rotten tooth.

*

*

The producer I slept with when I lived in Little Armenia sends a selfie from the top Grunion Canyon. The electrician I let call the shots once when I was a sleep-deprived assistant director sends pictures of his penis. The AD who threw radios at me when the batteries died, who I caught fondling former Miss Universe ██████████ in an overheated two-banger, tries to dispute my IMDB credits when they go through verification.

*

My mother keeps the signed *Time* magazine with *Platoon* on the cover in a locked drawer. I don't tell her he was high when he signed it. I know how much that issue means to her. We both know what it's like to be forced out of a dream.

To ▮▮▮▮. An oldie and a goodie. Thanks for the reminder.

I've kept things, too. I've built an archive of regret. I've framed pictures, laminated script drafts, made screenshots of all of the emails.

If possession of the truth is a crime, then book me for a felony—with the intent to distribute.

I refuse to let them get the last laugh.

I refuse to lose anything else.

*

I lost a child before it became a child. I lost a mother before I became a woman. I lost a childhood before I became a mother.

I'll never stop missing what has been taken from me.

*

▮▮▮▮▮▮▮▮▮▮▮▮▮▮▮▮▮▮▮▮▮▮▮▮▮▮▮▮▮▮▮▮▮▮▮▮

*

Do you know how many times a day ▮▮▮▮ touched my thigh in video village? How much porn ▮▮▮▮ bought and delivered to the EP on the daily? How often did ▮▮▮▮ laugh at the women trembling before the casting couch? Would Bob Dylan care that the man who wrote his liner notes trapped me in his house, threatened me against the deadbolt? Why didn't ██████, the VP of HR, respond to those emails I forwarded? The ones where he said he couldn't believe what he had done, that he couldn't live without me?

AND

How did two recovering alcoholics land a multi-million-dollar sitcom deal about a rapey white millionaire in active addiction? Why did it sell so damn well? W*hen* does the story about being sick start to feel good? W*hat* is the real cost of another drink? *Who* suffers the most? *Where* does pain go when the body is too full of suffering?

Ask who is responsible.
Ask why we pull down the stars and emblazon them with these names.
Ask how to hold evil accountable, at whose expense we let it entertain us.
Ask for the exact cost of a laugh.
(Answer: rampant, unpoliced complicity.)

*

██████████ is in black jeans, seated on the coffin-shaped Parnian. A sick and bloodless LA sky pulses through the window behind him in this executive office on the seventh floor of the Burbank building. The Stratocaster ████ ████ shreds when he is done berating his show's writers for weak tags and soggy cold opens is plugged in and humming. Every time I see it, I think about him dropping out of college and working his way up from nothing through the backdoor of animation, writing and recording theme songs for popular cartoons. How does a child's laughter turn into blood lust?

I tell ███████████ what happened. I omit nothing. I show him the text messages and the emails, explain the money and the touch. I tell him about the door, the anvil of ████'s body against me, the deadbolt, the debilitating fear.

After a long silence, ████████████ gets up. He circles the desk to his chair, hesitates next to the beloved Strat. He sits down and sighs, folds his small hands into a lazy kind of prayer.

"I'm so very sorry, kiddo," he says, and then, "Which department do you want us to move you to?"

*

Have you heard the story about the doctor who amputated the wrong leg, leaving the festering appendage intact?

Does anyone know his name?

*

"I'll send you wherever you want to go."

████████████ snaps his fingers.

The portal we have all heard about but haven't seen opens into the shape of a prism, spits Hollywood's red sunset across my face. The producer sizes me up. Will I slip through the scintillating threshold quietly, or will I have to be forced through, limb by severed limb?

A Lesson on Endings

September.

I tell her that good introductions are inverted fulcrums. They hook the reader by the ribcage and pull hard through the vertex. Good introductions don't hesitate. They prepare the reader for the body.

"Yeah," she says. "And then, the end."

"Conclusion," I say.

"Aren't those the same thing?"

"No," I say. "Arguments conclude. They don't end. That's the beauty of rhetoric. The conversations continue, even after you die. They never stop."

*

She sees me before I see her.

I'm not used to being seen. Not outside of the classroom. Living 40 miles from campus makes hiding from students easy.

But here she is: a jelly-sandaled cherub on one hip, a gingham-polo'd husband at her other. The white straw somerset is her trademark, a mainstay at the back of the classroom these first three weeks of the semester.

I don't have time to stuff the bottle under the driver's seat.

The look on her face. Recognition.

I don't know it yet, but she is about to save my life.

*

The disease wants me alone. The disease wants me dead. Every day. All day. In the middle of a lesson on synthesizing sources. During department meetings. After dinner. While I'm rinsing the shampoo from my daughter's hair.

Definitely tonight.

To keep from picking up, distraction is key. I pray, read, binge on sudoku. Obsession needs hands, so I keep mine busy. I pick up the phone. Scroll Facebook, TikTok, Pinterest. I open my laptop. Take an online quiz Violet bookmarked: "Which baby Pokémon are you?" Togepi, it would seem, and I can't disagree.

I accidentally open Outlook and read the email sent an hour ago at 2:43am.

I saw you at Target. I think it was a sign. I believe in signs.

I consider deleting the message and forgetting I saw it.

I have people to talk to, but I can't tell them anything.

My trembling fingers steady themselves against the keys. I type:

You tell me something, and I'll tell you something. That way, it's even.

Two minutes later:

I use heroin.

I keep at least two bottles behind a loose panel in our unfinished mudroom.

Her daughter is eight years old. My daughter is eight

years old.

She owns a Dutch Colonial with a detached two-car garage on three acres of farmland. I rent a half-remodeled Cape Cod near the oil refinery and seal the windows with plastic.

She wraps her arm with a silk belt from her daughter's My Little Pony pajamas. I wrap my bottles in plastic grocery bags and stuff them into gas station trash cans.

She dreams of meeting Macklemore and is teaching her daughter Mandarin. I distrust Nabokov and put my daughter to sleep with Golden's Field Guide to North American Birds.

She's twenty-five, a high school dropout majoring in political science. I'm forty-two, a career adjunct who isn't sure what she wants to be when she grows up.

Night finally releases its grip at 6am. Dawn's reveal is slow but honest. Our sugar maples, asters—the mailbox— all are planted firmly in the earth. The disease was wrong. The world never left us.

I have to get Ella up soon. Thank you for the company. I'm sorry I kept you up.

I don't flinch at my husband's footfall cracking down the oak stairs. I'm relieved to hear the hiss and sigh of water dribbling into the Mr. Coffee carafe. I write quickly.

No apologies. I couldn't sleep, and it helped me have someone to talk to. My office hours are at 5pm if you ever want stop by.
P.S. My favorite Macklemore song is "Starting Over."

*

I grade in the office with the empty name plate for an

hour before class. I drink cold coffee from a tumbler with the college's mascot of a hawk on the front of it and soften the corners of the room by putting lavender and lemongrass oil in the diffuser. The rhetorical precis are well-done and easy to mark, but only half of the class submitted them, so I finish up the nine I have by 5:40.

No one comes to visit me.

I gather up my effects, shoot two Bailey's minis, and make the short walk down the hallway to the computer lab I've been teaching in, on and off, for eight years.

The fire in my gut tells me this is going to be a good class, and when I get to GETCAM 116, Holly is there, waiting to be let into the classroom.

She looks so well-rested. So put together.

*

We are learning about logical fallacies and how to spot them when she stops showing up. The class feels half its size now, exponentially less curious and insufferably quiet.

I don't want to admit it, but I know how this goes.

*

October. A morning email:

Roxbury Treatment Center notified Academic Affairs that student #H237622 was admitted to inpatient for fourteen days and will return to class by October 30th. Please <u>do not drop this student from your roster during midterm confirmation of attendance</u>. Upon release and return to class, the student will arrange to meet with you and discuss work missed. You are encouraged to exercise flexibility and understanding, while still maintaining the integrity of your course policies.

*

I tell the students that transitions are easier than they sound, but they don't want to hear it. They want to leap between ideas like lily pads, run across four lanes of moving traffic. I tell them that if they can learn how to transition, they can create enough buoyancy to walk the reader across the water. They can build a footpath over the freeway.

*

November.

Daytime instructors rinse Tupperware in the metal sink and bitch about HR to the departing faculty secretary. The ancient copy machine, justifiably exhausted, releases a hearty dose of ozone as we cross the adjunct bay toward the rear office and close the door. I turn on the diffuser and offer her a lifesaver from a ceramic bowl my daughter made. I push aside a stack of calc exams another adjunct has left ungraded in a rush to get to the next gig.

Her cheeks are puffy from the suboxone, but her hazel eyes are bright and present. She thanks me for issuing the incomplete and promises to have the final draft of her visual rhetoric analysis—Macklemore's "Drug Dealer"— in before Christmas.

"I know you stan for 'Starting Over,' but," she smiles, "this song and I have a history."

Her sister is at Dickinson getting her masters in literature, and she plans to work with Molly on the revision. She tells me she is 38 days sober, and I tell her I can't remember the last time I had a drink.

"It feels so good to feel good," she says, twisting her wedding ring like a bottle cap. And then, "We got chickens last week and Ella named them after the Sesame Street characters. Grover is my favorite."

"I'm a staunch supporter of Bert and Ernie," I say.

"Yeah, but if you had to *Sophie's Choice* one of them—"

"Have you even seen that movie?"

"When I grow up, I want to be Meryl Streep," she says. "Hey, why don't you ever talk about when you worked in Hollywood? How you ended up here?"

I wait to cry until she leaves.

Lies fuel the disease. Lies keep you alone.

I want the perfect teeth and the Dutch Colonial. The multi-lingual daughter and the yard full of Sesame Street chickens. I want more years in front of me than behind so I can have time to *become something.* A person, at least. I want to be able to put it all down and do the right thing and clear my leger. I want to be sober, too. I want to live.

*

February in Pennsylvania is oppressive.

Tonight, the parking lot is all but abandoned. I let the students go early. The last one, a CNA off to her overnight shift at the assisted care facility near the Jennie Wade House, pulled out of the lot more than ten minutes ago, but here I am, idling in the dark like a hung jury. The Subaru's engine groans, exhaling dry heat into the driver's seat. In the rearview, the community college is a hopscotch of white light and swirling snow. The adjacent grocery store, closed for the incoming storm. Beyond my headlights and the berm and the road, Barlow Knoll is construction paper black. One hundred and fifty-eight years ago, it was the eruption site for the Battle of Gettysburg. Thousands bled and died there. I can't see it, but I can feel it. I've never felt it before. The collective suffering.

It's been 86 days since I've had a drink, but I'm white-knuckling it. The water heater flooded the basement. I lost my wedding band. The second-grade teacher says Violet needs to be screened for dyslexia and ADHD. I'm barely managing these new weekend preps at Penn State Harrisburg, where I'm hoping to get a foothold, anything to be delivered from the brutal cycle of night classes. Eight years. Eight fucking years. I am Sisyphus. I am done.

The air vent rustles the paper bag on the passenger seat. I thought I would come out of teaching rebuttals feeling renewed and able to defend myself against the bottle I picked up on the drive here. But I want that first drink now more than I want to be sober. Prayer, acceptance, reflection, and thinking through to the other side of the bottle are useless to me. I know that once I put it in me, I won't be able to stop. I can't stop once I start. And once I start, I can't stop starting. This helplessness— the wasted energy, the crippling obsession—is unbearable. Drunk or sober, the world keeps happening, and I am powerless.

A woman I know who knows a thing or two about a thing or two once told me that God has my number and will one day call me if he thinks I need to talk. Staring into the battlefield's darkness, I'm not thinking about God when my phone rings. But I will always think about God when I recall my husband's voice.

"Hey."

"Hey, what's up?"

"They found Holly's body last night."

"What?"

"And another person."

"Oh, my god."

"I saw it on the news. Minutes ago."

"Oh, my god."

"I thought you'd want to know."

"I just submitted paperwork to resolve her incomplete this morning."

"I know," he says. "You just finished class, right? Are you on your way home?"

"I'm...yes, leaving now. I had a student who needed to discuss his grade."

"Okay. Drive safely. It's squalling in Hanover."

"Oh, my god."

"I know. I'm so sorry. I love you. I'll be up when you get home."

*

Concession is part of the process. Sometimes, an argument is successful because it concedes the merits of the opposition. It accepts its own weaknesses.

*

May.

For my eight-year work anniversary, the dean gives me a hawk plush dressed in a maroon T-shirt with the college's acronym emblazoned in white across front. The penmanship in her handwritten note is symmetrical and controlled, the antithesis of my clumsy marginalia.

Eight years cracks the rubber-band movements of the heart.

It's eighteen hundred students and forty thousand miles on the odometer. It's one hundred and thirty thousand pages of writing, sometimes double-spaced, sometimes sans serif. It's two foreclosed rentals on opposite banks of the Susquehanna River and one Christmas at the Holiday Inn Express. It's three teaching excellence

THEY MORE THAN BURNED

awards and one blackout behind the wheel. Eight years is five tenure-track interviews, three published articles, one kindergarten graduation, two miscarriages, and a handful of relapses. It's countless churches, confessions, and second chances.

Eight years is a lighted match and the descending jar.

It's an ambush.

But it can be epiphany, too.

This morning: *I wake up.*

I drink coffee on our tiny porch in the dark with the bamboo wind chimes. It's early. The oil rigs haven't yet begun their daily parade down the pike. I whisper a prayer of gratitude and crawl back into bed. I tell my husband I love him with my entire body. I eavesdrop on my daughter's dreams while she sleeps.

At eight, Violet holds space for infinity.

At eight, Holly's daughter holds vigil.

I've been given the chance of another eight years.

*

If I could, I would tell her a conclusion is a reciprocal for the introduction. It births the reader, reformed by the musculature of the body's points, back into the world. It answers the questions: *So what? Why does this matter?* and *What should I do now?*

A conclusion is not an ending. It is synthesis of meaning. One can use an ending to create meaning, to draw a conclusion, to keep the conversation going.

*

September.

It is still light out when I pull into our driveway and park next to the asters, under the canopy of sugar maples.

Violet is swinging in the rainbow hammock beneath the treehouse my husband built when she sees me, *but I see her first.* In that split second before she parades toward me, I see the years I thought were behind me *right here, right now:* swinging beneath the treehouse, standing by the open car door, bowing to the earth, the late summer breeze. I kneel. Open my arms. I pull her into my heart. I thank God for today because it is all I have, and it is more than I ever imagined could be mine.

An Unofficial Meeting with the Network Executive Who Wants to Fund the Documentary about Your Life and RE-LAUNCH YOUR CAREER

INT. LA CIENEGA TAQUERIA - EVENING

TWO PEOPLE occupy a table beside the rolled-up glass doors of a hip Mexican taqueria in West Hollywood. Not that taqueria. This is a new one. With prism mosaic floors and a perimeter of glass tequila cabinets. All of the servers are dressed in black smocks with little silver agave patches on the pocket.

From our vantage ACROSS THE STREET, we PUSH IN, swoop over light LA traffic and SETTLE on the black iron railing separating our subjects from the busy sidewalk. It's Wednesday, just before SUNSET. This is the perfect spot for eavesdropping.

With his back to the entrance and the setting sun, LES ROBERTSON, 58, a silver-on-top, Armani-on-the-bottom network executive, sips a margarita on the rocks. Across from Les, AMBER FOLEY, 38, spoons a generous portion of guacamole into her mouth. Her vibe is present and engaging. She could be from LA but her age appropriated Coastal Grandma button-down and green turquoise sandals peg her for a Philly hipster or Berkshires-adjacent artist.

Les is unblinking, mesmerized.

                    LES
I've been to Carlsbad. A few
times.

                    AMBER
Oh, yeah? When?

                    LES
The first time? Let's see, it
was…2008? We were location
scouting for Real Housewives
of San Diego.

                    AMBER
I was in Burbank.

                    LES
Orange   County   blew   up
overnight, so we thought we
could convince the network to
split crews and spin off a San
Diego chapter. Scott wasn't
ever really on board with it,
and NBC was partial to New
York, which obliterated any
chances the San Diego chapter
had. Anyway, I wasn't there
long. I don't remember much
from that first visit. We spent
most of the weekend touring
beachfront properties by day
and reggae clubs by night. You
ever go to Winston's in PB?

                    AMBER
I wouldn't have pegged you for
a reggae guy.

                    LES
I'm actually a Springsteen and
sativa kind of guy.
        (then)
Was.
        (he laughs)
A lot changes in 20 years.

                   AMBER
I was a Titos and Tic Tacs kind
of alcoholic.

Les makes a sour face, deadpan slides his
cocktail glass away from her.

                    LES
I   think   you've   qualified
yourself enough tonight, young
lady.

We hold on LES—that creeping smile. Maybe
this isn't going to be like the other
times. Maybe this is the beginning of
Amber's moment. The first moment in a
series of significant moments…

                   AMBER
You said you visited more than
once. What were your other
visits like?

                    LES
I've been two other times. Once
with my ex-wife. We took the
kids to Legoland and the flower
fields. We ate some shitty food
at Pea Soup Andersen's.

                    AMBER
It's really not that good.

                    LES
Terrible.

                    AMBER
What about the other times?

                    LES
The other times were...after the
divorce. My son went to
boarding school on the beach
there.

                    AMBER
Army Navy Academy?

                    LES
That would be the one.

                    AMBER
I had boyfriends who went
there.

                    LES
Well, I won't ask how old you
were when you were dating ANA
boys. Considering I find you
very attractive and would love
nothing more than to have a few
unsupervised hours with you on
my deck in Malibu. I'd hate to
know if you and my kid ever
hooked up.

                    AMBER
         So that's all it would take to
         get the network to fund a
         project, huh?

                    LES
         Ha.

Off of Les's look, Amber backpedals.

                    AMBER
         Don't worry, Les. I'm just
         kidding.

                    LES
         Hey, I don't want to get in
         trouble. That #metoo shit is
         everywhere. And these jalapeno
         margaritas are next level. I
         blame the mezcal.

                    AMBER
         I'm glad. I was worried when I
         picked this place that it would
         be too hipster.

                    LES
         It's just enough hipster. Are
         you sure you don't want one?

Les points to his glass.

                    AMBER
         I'm good.

                    LES
         You're too young to be sober.

                    AMBER
I'm trying to start this new
fad. "Live smart. Die old.
Leave well-loved corpse to
science."

                    LES
Hmm. Well, I run three
marathons a year and have been
told I fuck like a porn star.

                    AMBER
Let's let hearsay be hearsay.

                    LES
Guess who's kidding now?

                    AMBER
The deadpan delivery really
got me.

                    LES
Truthfully, it's only one
marathon, and I've spent the
last two years practicing
tantric celibacy.

                    AMBER
Does that really work?

                    LES
          (shrugs)
Maybe you can tell me.

Amber shoves a heaping scoop of guacamole
into her mouth and watches Les watch her
with the intensity of a starving man.

                    AMBER
Les, why are you interested in
this project?

                    LES
Honestly? Currency. And, I
don't know. The zeitgeist.
Three years ago, CAA sent me
the proof of concept you edited
with the news coverage and
footage of those kids and your
Army friend. It was good. I
wanted to reach out, but I was
wrapped up in a climate change
doc down in the Falkland
Islands. When I got back, I saw
your short at Tribeca and was
just…floored. I hadn't seen
anything that raw and honest
since I can't remember when.

We hold on LES's face, filled with what
might be genuine emotion. A server's arm
dips into frame to deliver two small
plates of ceviche.

Amber struggles to maintain a confident
demeanor. The more hopeful she gets, the
more vulnerable she appears.

                    AMBER
                (nodding)
      I appreciate that.

                    LES
You're amazingly talented,
Amber.

                    (a beat)
          And really fucking hot.
                    (then)
          I can help you with more than
          the film you know.

Les sighs. Empties his glass.

                    LES (CONT'D)
          I'm usually able to hold my
          shit together around brilliant
          women much better than I am
          doing around you. I blame the
          jalapenos and mezcal.

Amber takes a long sip of water.

                    AMBER
          I feel like I don't know how to
          go about this.

                    LES
          There's nothing wrong with
          what we are doing.

                    AMBER
          What are we doing?

                    LES
          Having an unofficial meeting
          about   funding   your
          documentary.

                    AMBER
          I want to have an official
          meeting.

> LES
>
> We will. After the unofficial
> meeting.

Amber considers this.

> AMBER
>
> I can't believe your son went
> to ANA.

> LES
>
> And got expelled during
> convocation.

> AMBER
>
> Like father like son?

> LES
>
> I don't think I've ever known
> him enough to know him. And no,
> I was always a staunch rule
> follower. Contrary to this
> crippling moment of ostensible
> weakness—

A server's arm dips into frame to deliver
another jalapeno and mezcal.

> LES (CONT'D)
>
> I'm pretty dignified and
> moral.

Les recognizes he's making Amber
uncomfortable. He may be buzzed, but he
isn't stupid. But he doesn't change his
trajectory. He keeps pressing.

> LES (CONT'D)
>
> When you shot the initial

footage, you were, what, sixteen?

                    AMBER
Yeah.

                    LES
The other stuff, the stuff
what's his name shot—

                    AMBER
Danny.

                    LES
Yeah, Danny. Those tapes
weren't modified.

                    AMBER
No. We addressed that at the
end of They More Than Burned,
but it still came up in the Q
& A at Tribeca.

Les carefully sips the overfilled jalapeno
mezcal. He sucks the salt from his upper
lip.

                    LES
When you were sixteen. And
seventeen. Eighteen, nineteen—
before you left for film
school—did it ever feel like
there was something
supernatural about Carlsbad or
that house.

                    AMBER
Yellow House?

                    LES
Yeah.

                    AMBER
No.

                    LES
It didn't have a certain...feel?

                    AMBER
Of course it had a feel.

                    LES
Describe it to me.

                    AMBER
It felt like...

Amber takes a deep breath and closes her
eyes. She's going to be vulnerable in a
different way.

                    AMBER (CONT'D)
...the world was on fire and
there was nothing we could do
to stop it from burning except
hold it all in, as much of it
as we could, until—

                    LES
Until what?

                    AMBER
The flames ate us alive.

                    LES
What did that look like?

                    AMBER
A lot of things.
     (then)
I sometimes think it's still
burning. Even though so many of
us are...gone.

                    LES
There's a lot you're going to
have to cut out of the final
film.
                    AMBER
I know.

                    LES
What do you do with all of
that, all of the stuff you
can't fit in, the stuff people
won't permit you to tell?

                    AMBER
Oh, I don't know. Put it in a
book maybe.

                    LES
A memoir?

                    AMBER
People won't believe me if I
call it anything but fiction.

                    LES
Sure they will.

Amber throws Les a "how-would-you-
know?" look.

> LES (CONT'D)
> Do you know how much "reality"
> TV I've produced in the past
> twenty years? Thousands and
> thousands of hours. Most of it
> is shit. Your work? Not shit.
> The furthest thing from shit.

A beat.

> LES (CONT'D)
> There's nothing you can't make
> people believe if you make it
> look just so.
> (then, softly)
> I know you're still reeling
> from what happened with Peter
> at Warner Media. Yeah -- I know
> about it. But you gotta let
> that go. This --
> (he makes a "me-you"
> gesture)
> --is not Warner Media.
> (then)
> You know how to get them to
> believe you?

Amber concentrates on her half-empty water
glass, the BEADING CONDENSATION.

CLOSE ON LES'S FINGER

as he runs it down the side of the GLASS,
draws the beads of condensation together
into a STREAM that RUNS down the length
of the glass onto the lacquered wood,
where it SEPARATES into two bifurcated

tributaries that converge at the center: Infinity.

REVERSE ANGLE ON AMBER

considering Les and the power of his touch -- the water and its potential encryption. Is this a warning? A testimony?

BACK ON THE POOL OF WATER

and Amber's eye reflecting back at her. Infinite iterations of self-scrutiny in the form of a fractal.

We ZOOM into one of the pupils, enter the vitreous body, pass the spidery vessels into the retina, into the blank WHITE CANVAS of MEMORY, into the COTTON FIBERS OF THE CANVAS, splitting like the wooden plank of a capsizing ship, into which we dive deeper, into the dark, into a complex chain of glucose molecules until we reach

a single ATOM

incandescent, spastic, imperceptible in its shifting between anti-matter and being.

The atom is a PORTAL (not _that_ portal). It opens like a moonflower at nightfall. Fills with the taste of SAND, the texture of SEA. And the DIVINE SOUND of obsoletion: Memory.

THE OCEAN'S HORIZON stretches its fingers towards the edge of consciousness (or, in our case, the film frame).

Perfectly centered and gray, delineating ocean from sky, the horizon can hardly hold the weight of the clouds, pregnant and threatening, prepared to erupt in darkness.

In the LOWER THIRD of the frame, a small SWELL forms between a set of waves. We SLOWLY DESCEND TOWARDS IT. DURING --

> MAN'S VOICE (V.O.)
> (staticky, far away)
> *Sell it. Sell the shit out of it.*
> (then, closer)
> *Can you feel that?*

LEVEL with the horizon now, we PUSH IN towards the swell, watch it curl into a PERFECT WAVE, hurtling towards us, head-on.

> AMBER (V.O.)
> *I don't feel anything.*

SNOW, glittering and starlike, begins to fall into the sea, DISSOLVING the horizon and the sky, until all that is visible is the WAVE, continuing towards us, CRESTING --

> MAN's VOICE (V.O.)
> *That's exactly what it feels like to disappear.*

-- and then

with the velocity of a meteor

SHATTERS the screen into NONEXISTENCE.

A WOMAN GASPS FOR BREATH. Coughs a dry cough. A cough brought on by too much smoke.

OVER BLACK.

Amber's disembodied voice, devoid of ambiance, enters our mind like dream narration.

                    AMBER
        I'm still here.

                         SMASH CUT BACK TO:

INT. LA CIENEGA TAQUERIA - EVENING

The pool of water on the table. Les drawing the shape of infinity in the liquid. The soft wood SIZZLING. Steam rising from Les's finger.

Amber coughs, takes a deep breath of fresh air. CLICKCLICKCLICK CLICKCLICK. She looks around.

CLICKCLICKCLICKCLICK.

No one else seems to notice the SOUND of film perforations CLICKING through a projector, slowly drowning out the RESTAURANT NOISE.

CIGARETTE BURNS and DUST particles and HAIR start to clutter the previously pristine digital image. It becomes clear that we are watching Amber and Les on FILM. This scene has already happened. The fate of the narrative has already been determined and documented and platformed for us to watch, right here on this--

EVERYTHING surrounding Les and Amber SLOWS DOWN...

and then STOPS.

Waitstaff, diners, and LA traffic form a FREEZE FRAME backdrop for our principal actors. The mise en scène FLICKERS and FOGS UP as though, at one point during filming, light had leaked into the camera magazine, overexposing the image.

CLICK   CLICK   CLICK   CLICKCLICK CLICK

The SOUND of film CLICKING through the projector decelerates.

STOPS.

Amber and Les continue to operate in full-motion, DIGITAL CLARITY.

As the scene plays out, the edges of the film frame begin to BURN and MELT away, presumably from the heat of the PROJECTOR LAMP against the jammed image. Les and Amber, however, are not stuck. While the BACKGROUND catches FIRE and MELTS AWAY, they remain untouched. We PULL BACK, BACK, BACK until we are -

INT. EMPTY CINEMA - CONTINUOUS

-- watching the scene play out on a FILM
SCREEN. We continue to PULL BACK, reveal
the velvet-curtained Proscenium, pass
over rows and rows of empty seats, over
the back of a lone AUDIENCE MEMBER sitting
in the back row, watching, picking at her
popcorn.

ON THE SCREEN

The taqueria continues to burn away like
tissue paper, curling into oblivion until
it's just Les and Amber against white and
the CRACKLE of flames feeding on something
distant.

CLOSEUP on LES

pushing Amber's hair back. Caressing her
face. It's a bad film we've seen before.
One we don't intend to watch. But we can't
look away. We owe Amber this much. She
deserves to be seen.

                    LES
        I can make them believe you.
            (then, softly)
        Let me help you.

Amber opens her mouth, but the words are
either too slow to form or her lips have
forgotten how to shape resistance into
speech. Does she feel like this is her
only option? Does she feel like the quid
pro quo will be worth it this time? Even

after a lifetime spent fighting to remove her body from the bargaining table?

                              SMASH REVEAL:

THE LONE AUDIENCE MEMBER --

-- AMBER

in CLOSEUP. Disinterested in the film plot and gazing into the bottom of her nearly empty popcorn tub. She SHAKES it, rattles the last few popped and unpopped kernels around. The noise REVERBERATES across the empty theater.

ON THE SCREEN

Amber strikes a MATCH on the stone guacamole bowl and watches, with satisfaction, as the matchhead ignites and starts its slow journey down the wood. Les continues to caress Amber's face, completely blind to the flame. He doesn't see what we see: AMBER looking directly INTO CAMERA. Smiling at us. Making her decision.

                              CUT TO:

A WIDE SHOT OF THE DISAPPEARED TAQUERIA

of Amber pushing herself up from the table -- it is all that remains of the set - of Amber walking across the white space, TOWARDS CAMERA, until she is in CLOSEUP. She looks left and then right and then lights the edge of the film frame. She tosses the burning match INTO THE --

EMPTY CINEMA

where it lands on the floor and self-extinguishes.

BACK ON THE SCREEN

the flames eat through the film screen, lick at the Proscenium until the curtains IGNITE like tissue paper.

Amber, unconcerned, looks disappointedly into the bottom of the empty popcorn tub. Meanwhile, we

RISE into an AERIAL SHOT OF --

THE EMPTY CINEMA.

We watch Amber, small, dissatisfied but nonchalant, drift away from the encroaching INFERNO, down the long row of empty seats. She heads towards the emergency exit's smaller RECTANGLE OF LIGHT, which grows BRIGHTER and BRIGHTER as she gets closer and closer.

Behind her, the Proscenium CRASHES to the floor, scattering fire like glass from a broken window. Amber doesn't even flinch. She can't be bothered anymore. She tosses her empty popcorn bucket into a trashcan a few feet from the emergency exit as we --

CONTINUE to RISE, our OWN FRAME now catching fire.

If you wait a few more seconds, you might be able to see her step softly into the DAYLIGHT. You might have the inclination to call her name. Tell her you see her. That you saw everything. Go ahead. Watch her go. I'll give you just enough time for those gestures before I direct the fire to incinerate your screen, to burn this page, to obliterate the entire book and we --

SMASH CUT TO BLACK.

Acknowledgements

This book erupted like an underground fire unwilling to lie dormant any longer. Over three years of global devastation and uncertainty, it burned immeasurable emotional and creative acreage. What else did I have to do? Isolated with two young children and an immunocompromised spouse, there was only one action I could diligently perform: dig. Through Rubbermaid storage containers and old hard drives, through MiniDV tapes and cookie tins-turned time capsules, through high school yearbooks, deactivated URLs, and handwritten journals. It did not take long to discover the kindling that had been in my possession for more than two decades. The duress of a pandemic and desire for distraction from my debut collection's 31-month editorial schedule set me on a quest for fire.

I just didn't know it.

As I pieced my way through the papers and tapes and conversations I'd salvaged, the word "archive" kept writing itself on the backs of my eyelids, singeing my tongue. The French root of archive, *archif*, signifies evidence, specifically public record to be preserved. Archive's Greek etymology, *arche*, denotes a beginning, the elements of origin: air, fire, earth, water. In other words, *place* and all the things that comprise it. Aristotle took the origin model even further and argued that these elements include the ineffable substance of existence—the thing inside of the thing, the possibility a thing possesses simply by being.

Was the word archive nudging me towards place? Possibility? Preservation?

During the pandemic I "purged" the house of the surface-level old—paper things, clothing kids had outgrown, household tchotchkes we no longer needed—and then I *dug*. I emptied and arranged and stumbled over the artifacts of my longing until they made a shape: folded notes from friends no longer on this earth, low-fi video interviews I'd filmed months before and months after the towers fell, half a dozen old phones, full of texts and my late Gen-X despair. I dug up Y2K and post-9/11 disillusionment by the gigabyte, and as I spread it across my Steelcase, stacked it on my husband's rolltop—and lay it across the soft wood floors of our Cape Cod—I recognized a place that wasn't a place but a collection of material longing that evidenced a *potential* narrative—a narrative of *possibility*.

In Louise Varèse's translation of *Paris Spleen*, Charles Baudelaire writes, "[w]hat one can see out in the sunlight is always less interesting than what goes on behind a window pane [*sic*]. In that black or luminous square life lives, life dreams, life suffers." Baudelaire then goes on to describe a woman bending over, engaged in a house chore. From that, he imagines an indigent life of ceaseless, repeating hard labor. All of this from a single line of vision, a framed-in snapshot of a life. Buadelaire concludes that he "[goes] to bed proud to have lived and to have suffered in some one [*sic*] besides [himself]" and rebuts potential arguments against his interpretation of the woman's reality with "what does it matter what reality is outside myself, so long it has helped me to live, to feel that I am, and what I am?"

I used to employ this text (XXXV, "Windows") in class discussions as a means of encouraging writers and filmmakers to evolve beyond creative mimicry and translate their own sense of reality. Following the pandemic and the political turmoil of the past several years, however, I have humbled myself to the insidious implications of Baudelaire's flâneuring. One's reality and how they wield it—into narrative, into law, into systemic structures—*does* matter. Likewise, my use of personal artifacts and the archive I didn't know I was about to create *does* matter, particularly in how I contextualize it and frame it for consumption.

These are *fictions* drawn from the materials of my own life and observations. They are constructions. Possibilities strung together to create one vector of meaning. The only reality they convey is my attitude towards the cumulative essence—the *arche*—of the decayed zeitgeist that bore them.

There are always so many people to thank.

First, I have to thank Ariana Den Bleyker. It is no coincidence that our paths crossed, that you are the editor to publish this book. I cannot thank you enough for your kindness, honesty, care, and support. You are golden.

I would also like to thank the editors and readers where some of these works appeared in different forms previously: "Drive," *trampset*; "2001: Notes" (originally "2001"), *Pithead Chapel*; "Undertow," *X-R-A-Y Literary Magazine*; "17" and "Check Your Risk Level," *Maudlin House*; "Nine Bodies I Didn't Leave Behind" (originally "Seven Bodies I Didn't Leave Behind"), *Hobart After Dark*; "[redacted]" (originally "Punchline"), *JMWW*; "TAPE #21: 5/17/05" (originally, "Flashover"), *Still: The Journal*; "None of This Is Real," *Cutleaf*; "When an Alcoholic Falls from the Sky," *The McNeese Review*; "Work Release" (originally "Folding Elephants in Boiling Springs, PA"), *Twin Pies Literary*; and "A Lesson on Endings," *Porcupine Literary Magazine*. Special thanks to editors Hannah Grieco,

Marianne Worthington, Barrett Warner, Dave Housley, Shannon Wolf, Jo Varnish, and Mallory Smart.

In spite of a pandemic that tried to isolate us into obsoletion, my writing community flourished. So many people kept me alive emotionally, creatively—and with Instacart deliveries for when I had COVID and all other manner of COVID-related emergency illness. To my lifelines: DW McKinney, K.C. Mead-Brewer, aureleo sans, Shannon Wolf, and Hannah Grieco (again). I could not have finished this book or gotten through that horrible month (you know which one I am talking about) without your kindness and Door Dash/Instacart deliveries and postcards. To writers whose support has humbled me to smithereens: K.B. Carle, Dave Gregory, Barrett Warner (again), Kathy Fish, Jordan Windholz, Lannie Stabile, Francine Rockey, Daniela Sow, and Jackson Bliss. Thank you for always lifting me up, for helping me feel the expansive generosity of the writing community.

To all of my friends, scattered all across the country—in PA, in CA, in recovery—and around the world. But most importantly, to my dearest friend, Jennifer Kilgore. This book is dedicated to you.

I of course have to thank my parents, whose unflinching support of my need to write has kept me afloat through the theft of my Hollywood career, a near-fatal addiction and recovery, a recession, a pandemic, two cross-country moves, grad school, and parenthood.

To my children: Gillian and James. I love you. Unconditionally. 24 hours a day. Even when it's 4am and you are sleeping and I am awake, writing while you dream.

To my handsome Pennsylvania high school teacher, Rich: I love you. Without wax. Forever. With my eyes open.

About the Author

Tara Stillions Whitehead is a writer and filmmaker from Carlsbad, California. She received her BA in Cinema-Television Production from University of Southern California's School of Cinematic Arts and worked as a DGA assistant director before earning her MFA in Fiction from San Diego State University. Her work has appeared in places like *The Rupture*, *Cream City Review*, and *trampset*, and has been included in the Wigleaf Top 50 in 2021 and 2022, and was listed as notable in Best American Essays 2022. She released her debut chapbook/concept album, *Blood Histories*, with Galileo Press in 2021, and her second story collection, *The Year of the Monster*, released with Unsolicited Press, is a 2022 Maya Angelou Fiction Award and 2022 Aspen Words Award nominee. She currently lives and teaches in Central Pennsylvania, where she lives with her family and two cats.